Once Upon a Time in Tehran

*My dearest friend Carmela
Thank you for being such
a good friend.*

*Love you always
Shirin
26.06.12*

Shirin Amani Azari

Strategic Book Group

Copyright 2009
All rights reserved — Shirin Amani Azari

No part of this book may be reproduced or transmitted in any form or by any means, graphic, electronic, or mechanical, including photocopying, recording, taping, or by any information storage retrieval system, without the permission, in writing, from the publisher.

Strategic Book Group
P.O. Box 333
Durham CT 06422
www.StrategicBookGroup.com

ISBN: 978-1-60860-866-9

Printed in the United States of America

This book is dedicated to my daughter, Maya, my mother's other grandchildren, and those who enjoy learning about life through tales.

Acknowledgments

With many thanks to my husband, Paiam, for his patience and hard work at my side, and for believing in me when I didn't. A special thanks, too, to Dr. Josephine Klein, who was with me right from the start. Finally thanks to all those who supported me without knowing it.

In memory of my beloved mother, grandmother, Azadeh, and all those who touch us in magical ways in the short time that we are given to spend with them.

In tribute to Neda and all the Iranians who risked their lives in the name of freedom and in the hope of democracy in Iran.

1

"What time is it, Mum?" I asked as loud as I could while I had my head out of the kitchen window in case my uncle's green Paykan turned into the driveway without my noticing it first.

"It has been two minutes since you asked me last!" she shouted at me, perhaps because she didn't think I would hear it, having all my senses focused on our road.

Peculiar thing, time is! Why is it that time passes so slowly when we are waiting for something good to happen, like summer holidays, while the holidays or weekends always pass so quickly?

I wanted to share my thoughts with my mum but, one, I would have to at least bring in my head from outside the window in order for her to hear me; and, two, I have heard it all before. Like, "Time passes quickly when you have fun, and when you wait long you are waiting for something good." My favourite is, "When you have waited for something good and finally in the right time you get it, then you appreciate it even more."

"That is enough, Shirin. Your face has gone black from the smoke and air pollution." More to herself, she said, "Honestly, they behave themselves until their father sets his foot out of the door, and then their manners disappear with him. What are the neighbours going to…?"

I had forgotten all about my dad. He had flown to Andimeshk this morning. He left with his colleagues on an obligatory trip to provide medical help to the injured in the war camps based in southern Iran. I was worried for my dad, with thoughts like, *What if the camp he stayed at was bombed? What if this was the last time I saw my dad? What if he comes back but is injured or disabled for life? What if…?*

Focusing on something else must have made the time pass quicker because just then I heard my uncle's car horn as he turned onto the road. "Maman bozorg"—my mother's mother—"is here," I shouted, my head still out of the window. Then I shouted one more time when I managed to pull myself inside, just in case my mum and my brother hadn't heard me.

I opened the patio window and shouted one more time so that Meme (my special name for my father's mother) and Babee (grandfather—my father's father), who lived on the first floor, and Amoo (uncle—my father's brother in Farsi), who lived on the third floor, could hear me before they heard the doorbell. I was downstairs and had the door open before my mother could push the *ef-ef*—intercom—to open the door.

There she was with a big smile on her kind face. She was still wearing those big black eyeglasses that Mum had warned her about last time. She was comfortable wearing them, she had explained, and also that she has had them for a long time and it would be like giving up a part of herself. Of course Mum disagreed; she said that with every ending there was a new beginning.

I don't know if I would even recognise her without her glasses. I have always seen her with those glasses on her. It is a part of her. I don't want anything about her face to change. *Whew—what a relief,* I suddenly thought. *She is as I remembered her to be.* With a feeling of relief, I threw myself in her arms.

"You look so nice," I said.

"I look the same!"

By this time my brother, Shahin, who had caught up with us, greeted my grandmother, as did Dayee (mother's brother in Farsi—uncle), while wiping the kisses off his face.

"How many days are you going to stay with us?" I asked

"Dayee has to go back soon, but I will stay with you for a month."

"Until Dad gets back?"

Maman bozorg nodded and the smile was back on Shahin's face. We could hear Mum moaning as she met us halfway to join us.

"I don't understand them today. Shirin should know better—she is the oldest. Lunch is almost ready—and Mum, we will talk about those shoes later," my mother said to Maman bozorg. I looked at my grandmother's comfy flat shoes and couldn't see anything wrong with them. She always chose flat shoes because she was tall and didn't want back problems, she had said in her defence.

2

"In a minute, I'm coming," Maman bozorg said, hearing me call for her from my room.

There had been so many thoughts and feelings about how we would agree on the sleeping arrangements that now that we had finally agreed on them I didn't want to wait any longer. It was past eight o'clock anyway and Shahin was fast asleep. Honestly, he would drop anywhere as soon as the time reached eight.

I remember once, in a family gathering, people adjusted their watches because Shahin had fallen asleep (as usual) at exactly eight and surprised some whose watches were too fast or too slow.

"If I wouldn't have known any better, I would have thought that your mother gave birth when she was only seven months pregnant with you," Maman bozorg said, shaking her head.

I never understood that expression. Apparently it means that if someone is too impatient or eager, it is because they couldn't wait for the nine months of the pregnancy process. The baby forces him/herself out of the mother's womb after only seven months?

"I can't believe that I have agreed to sleep in your room on the floor, between you and Shahin," Maman bozorg said in a lowered voice, looking at Shahin.

"What is wrong with that?" I defended myself.

"Nothing, except the fact that there are there two perfectly comfortable beds in this room and one waiting for me in my room"—the guest room—"and your mother is lying in her own bed on her own," Maman bozorg almost whispered while taking her socks off.

Who else would she be sleeping with? I thought. *My dad is away.* But this was no time for jokes or sarcasm. I had been waiting for this moment long enough.

"*Yeki bood, yeki nabood…*" (Once upon a time.) I could feel my heart racing, wondering which story Maman bozorg was going to tell me this time—or perhaps there could be one that she hadn't told me before.

> Once upon a time there was a happy couple living in a beautiful cottage far, far away. They had everything they wished for and were very happy together, but had been feeling the longing for a child more lately than before.
> Finally, after seven years, on a summer day the beautiful lady of the house told her husband that they were to be expecting soon. Every day went like months, every month like years, but the excitement of becoming parents was far too great and they enjoyed every day of it.
> The day came when the baby was ready to be delivered, and with her husband by her side the midwife helped her give birth to a beautiful baby girl they named Ziba. They held Ziba

between them, thinking and saying, without using any words, that she looked exactly like her mother.

Unfortunately Ziba didn't have the chance to see what her father meant when he spoke of her beloved mother.

"What happened to her mother?" I asked in denial.

"She was tired from the difficult labour, so she needed her rest and was not disturbed during the night when the baby cried of hunger. She passed calmly into the other world."

"How unfair!" I cried.

"Wait until you hear the rest."

Ziba grew up to be a beautiful young lady, who loved her father more than life itself. She missed having a mother around. Even though she didn't have a chance to get to know her mother, nor did she even know what having a mother would be like, she still missed something in her life—which she felt must be motherly love.

Sometimes her father would say to Ziba, 'This is exactly what you mother would say,' or 'You scratch your nose exactly like your mother.' Ziba often wondered about her mother and looked in the mirror to see if she could see her mother in herself as much as others could.

One day, late at night, there was a knock on the door, and Ziba, much to her surprise, rushed to open it—even though her father had warned her about opening the door to strangers. She was excited to see who it could be, as usually no one passed their path.

There was a young girl about the same age as Ziba and a lady who seemed to be her mother, both soaking wet in the rain. They asked politely to stay the night as they couldn't find their way in the dark.

They stayed the night, then a week, then a month, and months after that. Eventually the woman moved from the guest room into the master bedroom and became Ziba's step-mother, and Shamsi, who was a couple of years younger than Ziba, became her step-sister.

Ziba did most of the chores around the house because she was familiar with a lot of things, like where to get the logs, how to get them, where to get the water, where to get the fresh vegetables, and so on.

After awhile it became more of a habit and Ziba had to sleep closer to the door in the kitchen so she would not wake up the rest of the house when she went out to get the water and do the daily shopping. Shamsi eventually moved into Ziba's bedroom and didn't feel the need to help out with the chores around the house.

Ziba hadn't seen her father this happy for a long time, and therefore went along with the silent agreement that she would do the housework. In the meantime, Shamsi isolated herself, and because of this isolation she lacked social skills and confidence. She ate and grew in size, but seemed to get hungrier the more she ate.

The step-mother never seemed to be satisfied with anything. She criticised Ziba's father for a lot of things, and Ziba could sense that her father was withdrawing more and more, like Ziba had done, spending most of his days out of the house and leaving the mother and daughter to their eating. Of course Ziba missed her father, but they hadn't spent much time together lately, and Ziba knew how much her father appreciated breathing space from the dysfunctional family.

One early morning while Ziba's father was away for business, Ziba took a piece of loaf, wrapped it, and put it in her *boghcheh* (lunch pack) along with some sugar, and with her two empty buckets sneaked out as silently as possible and headed for the well.

The beauty of nature allowed her to be philosophical about life and the living. She enjoyed the singing of the birds, their whispering to their babies, telling them about life, what it would feel like to grow up and fly. She could stand and watch the squirrels play, tease each other, and then run from a fox that would hide behind a tree.

'Can you help me, young lady? I haven't eaten for days,' she vaguely heard someone pleading behind her.

Ziba looked down and there she was—an old lady curled up, holding her stomach as if she had a stomach ache. Ziba removed the loaf she from her *boghcheh* and gave the old lady half of it.

'I have enough to eat until I get back home,' Ziba thought.

'Can I have some water? I haven't eaten for a while. I better soak my throat before I eat!'

'I am on my way to get water from the well,' Ziba said. 'I can come back this way and bring you some water.

'Sit down and keep me company,' the old lady demanded carefully. Ziba knew that she couldn't afford to sit down if she had to get the water, come back this way to bring her some of it, then get home to prepare dinner for the household. She was expecting her father back this evening.

'It seems that you have been lonely for a time and longing for company, but I am expecting my father this evening and I have to…'

'Isn't it interesting that we go through life without standing still for a moment to look at how we are living and what makes it worth living?' the old lady asked.

Ziba looked at her, thinking that she must have plenty of time on her hands if she could be so philosophical about life. She felt that she would like to share her thoughts with the old lady, as she seemed wise. Ziba remembered the times she spent with her father late at night talking about life outside their village, miracles of life and sometimes about death.

'Tell me about you! Enlighten me, young lady,' the old lady said.

Ziba told her about losing her mother at birth, about her father, and how Shamsi and her mother entered and festered themselves in her home, and how she was now a maid instead of a family member.

The old lady seemed understanding and empathetic towards Ziba's feelings, and it felt good to Ziba and made her want to stay longer, but eventually she had no choice but to leave.

Ziba came back later that day with the water, and in the days that followed did she she not only bring food and water for the old lady, but exchanged ideas about life and living. Ziba felt that the old lady knew too much to have lived her life in the village. She was wise and seemed like a traveller, but she had chosen not to talk about herself and Ziba respected that.

'What do you think you would do if you had enough money to buy the whole village seven times over?' the old lady asked one day.

'What a strange question,' Ziba thought. 'I don't know! I don't even know how much money I'd need to buy the village one time over.' Ziba thought about it for awhile, then said, 'I have never had much money and throughout my life I have had my good days, better days, bad days and worse days. One thing is for sure—money has never made a day any better for me. I may have received a gift now and then that gave me temporary joy, but believe me when I say that it was temporary.'

The old lady lifted her coat for the first time and mumbled, 'I think it is time to show you this.'

Ziba was blinded by the jewellery—the diamonds, rubies, gold, and stones in every possible colour that she didn't even know the names of. It took awhile before she could pull herself together. 'What do you mean it is time to show me this?' Ziba gently asked.

'I was left this jewellery to give to someone who doesn't really need it or isn't looking for it. You wouldn't believe what some people go through to get their hands on money. They cheat, lie, steal—and sometimes they even kill each other for it. If you find happiness without money, it is only then that you are actually capable of handling the money that is given to you.' She took two hands full of jewellery and gave them to Ziba.

'I can't accept this,' Ziba said. 'I'm not frightened to accept your generosity and kindness! I just don't know what to do with it.'

'When you least expect it, it will come to use. Now I must tell you something before we part.'

'Are you parting with me?' Ziba asked.

'It is time for me to move on. I am needed elsewhere. I am leaving this afternoon, so you don't have to come back this way today. You have to go back the other way from the well like you did before you met me.

'On your way back you will meet challenges that you will need guidance with, so listen to me carefully. When you get your water take the path straight home. Do not look back, whatever you do. There will be different voices to try and challenge you to look back or towards the direction of the voices. Don't give in to the challenges—just look straight forward and they will eventually give in. And remember—do not tell anyone about this.

'Now it is time to say goodbye.'

On her way to the well, Ziba was thinking about how they had met and wondered whether it had been a coincidence or fate. Had the old lady been from this world? Was she human? Who would give someone so much jewellery for water and some bread? What was she going to do with the jewellery anyway?

She filled the buckets with water and hid the jewellery equally in her pockets and clothes and headed home. She was thinking about the voices the old lady had mentioned and the challenges that she was going to face when suddenly she heard a child's cry. The farther away from the well she got, the louder the cry. She wanted to look to see if a child was actually crying. Perhaps a child actually needed help, but she kept reminding herself of what the old lady had told her.

Suddenly the cry turned into a woman's angry voice: 'Is your heart made of stone? You don't respond to a child's cry for help! Look at me when I talk to you.' Ziba walked forward and focused on the path in front of her.

Soon the voices changed—one a woman in agony, and the other a man's demanding voice, who talked as if he was God himself. Ziba could se the cottage now and knew that this misery would be over soon.

'Ziba, I am so glad that you're home.' She recognised her father's voice. "I have been waiting for you. Look at me Ziba and see what happened to me on my way home from the journey.'

Ziba wanted to turn around and have a look at her father, but she stopped herself, wondering why her father was talking to her from behind when the house was in front of her. He wasn't even expected back until this evening. She decided not to look back and move forward. She could see the cottage, so she could soon find out whether the voice was actually her father's.

'Whatever happens, do not look back,' were the old lady's words. She decided to trust her.

The closer she got the door, the weaker the voices became in tone, although they were more abusive. 'Is this how I brought you up to be? Disrespecting your own father and not responding to him—especially when he asks something of you?'

But the voices gradually faded, and as soon as she held the door knob to the cottage they stopped altogether. She opened the door, rushed inside, and breathed out a sigh of relief, as if she had been holding her breath the whole time.

'Who are you running from?' Shamsi asked with her mouth full.

Ziba looked up and saw Shamsi sitting at the kitchen table with her legs crossed, holding a half-eaten apple, with the other half in her mouth, passing it from her left cheek to her right cheek in an attempt to chew it. 'What do you mean?' Ziba asked as she tried to straighten her clothes and brush off the unusual challenge she'd just faced.

Little did she know that as she fussed with her clothes a piece of red ruby rolled down her skirt on to the kitchen floor and stopped at Shamsi's right big toe.

'Mum,' Shamsi yelled out without a hesitation. Ziba wanted to hush and shush her, but there was no point. As soon as Shamsi picked up the ruby from the floor, she started strip-searching Ziba and investigating her.

The humiliation was more than Ziba could stand, especially when she was accused of lying after she had told them the whole story. Then the beating started. She couldn't blame them for not believing the story, as she could hardly believe it herself.

After she was stripped of her clothes, the jewellery, and her dignity, she was left to bleed while the mother and daughter would decide what to do.

'You are lying to us because you don't want us to get our hands on the treasure that you have either found or stolen and now hidden somewhere for yourself. There is only one way to find your hidden treasure. I will send Shamsi out to follow your path to the well to see what she can find,' the stepmother said at last.

'I can't go, Mum! I have never left the house. I wouldn't know where to go and what to do. What if an animal attacks me or I get beaten by people?' Shamsi wailed.

'You will go no matter what! No one will ruin the chance of this wealth for me, not even you.'

'We have enough anyway, Mum. Ziba said that it was all she was given...'

'Ziba said, Ziba said. The girl has been so isolated that she has probably created her own fantasy world anyway. How do we know that this is all of the jewellery? There must be more, and why stop now when we can get more? Leave now or you'll end up bruised like Ziba.'

Shamsi was given a piece of bread and some water and literally pushed out the door. She tried to look ahead to face her fear, but soon realised that this was the first time that she had been out on her own. She tried to stop shaking by stroking her arms, as she could picture herself being the main course at a wolf's feast tonight. 'They can probably already smell me,' she thought.

She could also hear her own stomach trembling. All that talk about the food made her hungry. She remembered that she had a piece of loaf in her *boghcheh*. She also remembered that her mother had said something about keeping it, but couldn't remember for what reason.

Wrestling with her thoughts, she decided to take a small piece of the bread and chew on it. That small piece didn't last her long, and soon she craved another piece.

'No one will notice anyway. It is only a small piece and I am going to keep the rest. My mother doesn't want me to starve anyhow,' she kept reassuring herself.

She wasn't sure what she was supposed to look for, but she looked around to see if there was anything interesting. Suddenly she saw something white and round between a couple of trees. Hoping that she'd found the treasure so that she could go home soon with the mission accomplished, she threw herself on it.

To her astonishment the white and round thing turned out to be a mushroom. She looked closely at it and picked it up.

'It may not be a treasure to my mother, but to me...' she thought, and took a bite of it. 'Mmm—it is heaven,' she said aloud.

She needed to wash it down with some water, realising she'd better not finish it all because she had a bit to go yet. How long did she have to go anyway? She couldn't believe that her mother actually put her through this. Didn't her mother always say that blood was thicker than wine? Shamsi thought that meant that she was more important to her mother than luxury.

The more she thought about this the angrier she got. 'I can't believe she did this to me. I might as well get lost and end up as the food of wolves. I don't know my way in the woods, I've never been out on my own, and as soon as she saw those shining stones she kicked me out to find more or die. I might as well sit here and wait for the animals to attack me,' she whispered hopelessly to herself.

One thing was certain—all that talk about food had made her hungry again, so she took out the rest of the bread, ate it, and washed it down with the rest of the water. 'I must be close to the well anyway,' she thought.

'Young lady, do you have any spare food for a starving old lady?' Shamsi heard a voice pleading. She looked down and saw a lady curled up not far from her under the tree.

'Who are you?' she asked the old lady.

'What does it matter who I am? I am old and thirsty. Can you find it in your heart to offer me some water?'

Shamsi remembered why she should have kept the bread and the water. It all seemed to fall into place now, about what Ziba had sworn was the truth. There was indeed an old lady asking for food and water.

'I don't have food or water,' Shamsi said. 'But you are going to give me the jewellery because if you don't my mother will kill me and you both.'

'Can you bring me back some water from the well?'

'Are you deaf, woman? I don't have anything and I am not going to any well to get anything for you. You are going to give me the jewellery or I will take it from you. Seriously—women like you make me sick, having all that money and yet you beg for food and water.'

'I will give you all I have left—you seem to need it more than I do,' the old lady said. 'Go to the well, which is not very far from here, and take the other way back. On your way back you will hear voices who will call out for you. If you don't look back you will be able to keep the jewellery.'

Shamsi took the last bit of the treasure, hid it carefully in her clothes, and made her way to the well. From there she headed home. As soon as she left the well she began to hear the voices. The farther away from the well and closer to home she got, the louder the voices would get, asking for help, directions, and begging to be saved from evil. Shamsi walked towards the cottage and focused on walking forward. Suddenly she heard the voice say, 'Shamsi, I have a nice juicy apple for you, but I guess you don't want it because you just had a mushroom and bread.'

Shamsi remembered the apple she had earlier—red, juicy, and sweet, just the way she liked it. She could almost taste it now. The more she thought about it, the more her mouth watered.

'You know you want it!' the voice said.

'I will turn around and grab the apple and run a fast as I can,' she thought—'and besides, I am very close now and can almost see the door.'

She turned around, expecting to see somebody offering the promised juicy red apple, but instead she was stripped of the jewellery by the wind, as if it had a life of its own. Shamsi could see every one of the shining stones disappear with the wind. There wasn't enough time to reflect over what had happened—the next thing she knew was that that same wind hit her in the forehead and knocked her backwards.

Her head felt heavy and she didn't dare to look around—and she didn't want to stay around for the next thing to happen, so she focused on the door of the cottage and slowly but surely made her way there. She knocked on the door and fell unconscious, both out of fear and exhaustion. She opened her eyes when she felt slaps on her cheeks and heard her mother's angry voice.

'Wake up! Wake up, for goodness sake! We have to leave before he gets back—we have to leave now, in the dark. It is best to leave in the dark. No one can see you like this.' She was crying.

None of this made sense to Shamsi, but the thought of leaving again made her ill. She couldn't leave—not now, not ever. She wanted to tell her mother what had happened to her, but her mother seemed to be preoccupied with her own thoughts.

'I can't believe that I forced you out in the woods. You must understand, Shamsi—it was not my fault. I wanted this for you. I wanted us to have a secure future with the money. Well, what is done is done now. I have already packed a bag of necessities and all the jewellery Ziba had brought home so that we can leave before your step-dad gets home tonight. We don't have much time to waste.'

'Mum, you don't understand! I am physically unable to leave. I am too ill to even tell you what happened to me today.'

'You are the one who doesn't understand, Shamsi. You don't need to tell me what happened to you today because I see it all on your face. Maybe this will help you to understand as well,' she said as she handed a mirror to Shamsi.

Shamsi could barely sit up to look at herself in the mirror. Her head still felt very heavy. She tried to half-sit and looked in the mirror. She saw a difference at first, but couldn't really put her finger on it. When she looked closely, she saw something on her forehead that she hadn't seen before. She looked closer, but couldn't figure out what it was, so she touched it. Then, in the attempt to pull it off, her forehead almost came with it.

'I have already tried that—it is not coming off,' said her mother. 'I have even tried to cut it off, but it is impossible. We have to leave in the dark so that no one can see you like this. Then we have to find a doctor or someone somewhere in the world who can help us remove that thing from your forehead.'

There was no need for any more persuasion. Shamsi followed her mother to the door, trying to cover her forehead with a scarf. She quickly realised that it was impossible to cover—no matter what she did it stuck out.

'Mum, what is it on my forehead?'

'Hopefully I am wrong about this, but it looks like a bull's penis.' That was the last Ziba heard from them.

I kissed my grandmother goodnight, but I couldn't stop thinking about Ziba and the money that brought her happiness, and the fact that Shamsi and her mother now had to spend the money to travel the world just to find someone who would probably (if there was even such a person) charge them a fortune (if there was even any money left by the time they found that person) to get the thing off her face.

"God acts and moves in mysterious ways," my grandmother used to say, and it wasn't until now that it started to make some sense.

3

"Where is Maman bozorg?" I asked as soon as I opened the door.

"She is taking a nap," my mother answered, pointing to the guest room.

Isn't this fantastic? I thought. *I just come home, and there she is, living in our home with us. I shall cherish every moment and make the most of it.*

"Not so fast, young lady!" I heard Mum shout as she spotted me on my way to check on grandmother. "She has just gone in to take her afternoon nap—and besides, you know the rules: no stories until you have finished your homework.

She was right. I had loads of homework to do, but no one seemed to understand that Maman bozorg would only stay until my dad's return. Before we knew it, days would fly away and we would have to say goodbye. Ashkan (my dayee's son) was so lucky, having my grandmother living with them. Ashkan was only two months younger than me and one of my best friends (and —at times I saw him as my worst enemy). But deep down I knew that he was the best cousin anyone could ever wish for.

I was so relieved when I realised that there were only a couple pages of homework left. I must have set a new record the way I wrote the answers to the questions we had been given today. *I just hope that our teacher can read them, because I sure can't,* I thought as I looked at my own handwriting. "Writing quickly can affect your handwriting—in a bad way," was Susani Khanom's motto. Perhaps she had a point!

"Can I come in?" my mother asked and walked in before I had time to get my papers together and hide the evidence of my poor effort to finish my homework. "Have you almost finished?"

"Yes!" I answered and swallowed my saliva, afraid she'd ask me to have a look at it.

"Shahin has a high temperature and it won't go down. It is best if I take him to the hospital. Your amoo will accompany us to the hospital. We will get back as soon as we can, but in the meantime I want you to be a good girl and be in charge until we get back."

I could hear a singing voice in my head. I was so over the moon about being on my own with Maman bozorg that I totally forgot about my brother's temperature. He was a sweet child that everyone wished was theirs as soon as they saw him. He was a dream child who people thought only existed in a dream world. He had big green eyes, fair skin with rosy cheeks, and a big smile on his face. He didn't make any trouble, nor did he speak much. But when he did he made sense, and he had a good sense of humour.

"I am going to the hospital, Shirin. If we leave now hopefully the doctor can see me before I fall asleep," he said, yawning.

An hour later I was finished with all of my homework and walked into the living room to see what my grandmother was up to. To my astonishment I found her sitting in the dark in the kitchen, smoking her Zar cigarettes.

"Smoking kills, you know!" I whispered, trying not to disturb her deep thoughts.

Maman bozorg only smoked when she was under a lot of stress and pressure. Was something seriously wrong with my brother? Perhaps something had happened to my dad that my mother hadn't told me about. All of a sudden I felt sad and swallowed my tears. I had to build up my courage to ask her about it. She wouldn't hesitate for a minute to tell me what was on her mind.

"Maman bozorg," I called as I turned on the lights.

"Turn the lights off," she yelled. "On the news this evening they said that Iraqi military planes are flying over Tehran. They said that we should turn the lights off, and as soon as we hear the siren we should move down to the lowest level of the house."

"You mean the city siren?" I said and looked at my grandmother with panic as she took another puff of her cigarette.

"Well, we can't expect your mother and brother to come home until all of this has calmed down. I just hope that your dad is well and safe," she responded calmly.

I was gasping for air at this point.

"I can tell you about the time…" she began.

"This is no time for stories," I said harshly. It must have been the first time I have ever said that, which meant I really must have been scared. "You are right about Mum and Shahin," I continued. "They are safer in the hospital and they will be taken to the basement for the safety of the staff and patients." My father had told me about this some months earlier, after the first Iraqi attacks on Tehran.

"My father will call us as soon as he can," I added, "because he must have heard about this before we did, and you know Dad—he is generally worried about everyone and every thing, especially his family.

"As for you and me, we are going downstairs to Meme and Babee's flat," I said as I put my slippers on.

"We are not going anywhere, young lady."

"Yes we are! My mother put me in charge, and as someone in charge I have decided that to be safe we are going to the lowest level of the building, and that happens to be my grandparent's apartment."

"That's funny, because I remember your mother putting me in charge, even though she didn't have to because I am older, wiser, and have earned the title."

"Let me see if I have understood this correctly: you are in charge of our safety for various reasons, and even though you heard the siren and hear the noises and planes from outside, you are suggesting that we should sit here and wait for everything to blow over?"

"When your time comes, it comes," she said, shaking her head.

"You are responsible for me, though—you are in charge of my safety. You need to keep me safe, and at the moment I am not."

"You and your tongue. Will you be safe downstairs?"

"Yes! Everyone knows that you are safer on the lowest level. Even you told me that Baba Bozourg (my mother's father) said that in earthquakes they were told to get themselves to the lowest place—if possible, in the basement."

§§§§§

"Khanom Jaan,"—Dear Lady—"it is so nice to see you! Welcome to our humble place! To what do we owe this pleasure?" Meme greeted Maman bozorg and called for my Babee.

"Enough! Let's go in and then you can talk. I don't want to die in the hallway, and keep your voices down," I whispered, pushing both of them inside.

Meme looked at both of us with confusion and seemed to be waiting for an explanation.

"Khanom Jaan," Maman bozorg called out in a pleading voice, "I heard the news warnings about the Iraqi attack, and ever since Shirin heard the alarm she has been acting weird."

Meme and Babee both looked at me with surprise.

"Didn't you hear the siren? Don't you hear the explosions from outside?"

"The explosions are far away from here," my Babee said calmly. "Let me put the radio or the TV on so you can hear," he added, then went to turn on the TV.

"No," I screamed, yet trying to keep my voice down out of fear. "They will hear us. Didn't you listen to the news? They said that we need to take precautions. People have painted their car lights dark blue in case they are outside when the city siren goes off, their windows are taped across in case there is an explosion, the curtains are in dark colours, and the lights are turned off when the siren goes off."

I knew where I would find a candle, found it, brought it and asked Meme for the matches, lit it, placed it on the table, and quickly turned all the lights off.

"I remember hearing on the news that you should keep yourselves in the corners of the houses because it is safer, and I remember something about standing up. Yes, standing up in the corners of the houses—like this!" I said, then demonstrated by standing in one of the corners.

"Can I offer you some tea, Khanom Jaan?" Meme asked, looking at my Maman bozorg and ignoring me totally.

"This is not a courtesy call! We are refugees in your house, seeking safety and escaping death," I said softly.

"Yes please," Maman bozorg replied to Meme's question while looking at me as if she wanted to make a point.

"That's just great! My father is in the middle of the attacks, my mother and brother are God knows where, and for all I know you could be the people I'll be stuck with forever—and not only don't you care about your own safety, you couldn't care less about mine."

On that note all three of them chose their own corner without saying a word, as if they had mutually agreed which corner was theirs.

After fifteen minutes of that silence, standing with our backs to the cold walls in the dark, my Babee decided to sit on a chair in the corner, and soon both of my grandmothers followed suit.

I, in the meantime, was too scared to move. The explosions seemed to get closer and louder. I was thinking about my father and why he had not yet called, and my mother, who should have called by now. I wondered if they had even reached the hospital before the siren sounded.

"Khanum Jaan, how is Nader?" Meme whispered, asking about my mother's only brother and looking at me for approval of her tone of voice.

"Well, he was unwell last week and I didn't know…"

"Shush!" I almost yelled. I couldn't believe my ears. "Can't you just sit still and be silent for a moment? You always scold us children for not being able to do so, yet you are worse."

Ten minutes later the sounds of the planes was less regular, and I decided to sit on the floor where I'd been standing, just to give my feet a rest. As soon as I sat down I heard something, and not only did I stand up but I ordered the others to do so as well. Soon I realised that it was false alarm, so I sat back down, but again I heard something and I had to stand up in case the roof collapsed over our heads. Because this happened over and over, my grandparents gave up on my hunches and false alarms, which seemed pretty real to me at the time.

As I continued the routine of sitting down and almost immediately standing up again, I heard my Maman bozorg say, "This must have been the vision of the yo-yo creator."

Everyone burst into laughter, and I didn't even have the energy to hush everyone.

"You seriously look like a yo-yo in human form," Babee agreed.

We realised that the Iraqi planes had left by that time, and that the street lights were back on, so we anxiously put the TV and radio on to hear the latest news.

For the rest of the evening, after my mother and brother's safe return, I could hear Maman bozorg laughing with my mother while demonstrating my gestures, and later my mother telling my father on the phone and painting him a picture while laughing together about it. I eventually learned to laugh about it too, but at the time it seemed very real to me.

4

I spent the next couple of days studying for a history exam, and I didn't get to spend much time with my family. I missed sitting with my mother and Maman bozorg in the evenings, the scent of freshly brewed tea and Maman's famous saffron *halva*.

It was difficult to concentrate when I could hear them talking and laughing while drinking tea and cracking nuts. I envied Shahin, who was in his first year, with minimal homework, and could at least watch a video until his bedtime.

I will be free tomorrow, I reminded myself, *and I will enjoy my freedom by celebrating my weekend by watching videos, eating grandmother's home-cooked meals, freshly baked Danish pastries from the local bakery, fresh roasted nuts, and drink a lot of freshly squeezed...*

"Shirin," I heard my mother calling out, breaking the thread of my thoughts. "Maman"—Mother (that's what she called Meme)—"is calling for you from the patio."

Meme told me that she had a surprise for me, so I headed down the stairs. When she says that, it usually means she has a warm glass of milk for me, which I hate the taste of. But I drink it out of courtesy because, one, it is supposed to be good for me, and two, because she goes through the trouble of heating it up for me. So drinking it was the least I could do. I have to admit that I do enjoy my afternoon visits with Meme, even if it means that it has to be over a warm glass of milk.

As usual I sat down and poured my heart out about my exam in the morning, and how much effort I had been putting into studying for it, and that I missed being with my family even though I was living with them. As usual she told me that it would be useful for me in the future to learn and know my subjects—especially history.

Then she went into the kitchen, and I could hear the sound of the fridge door open.

Hasn't she heated up the milk already? I don't have time for this, I thought.

She came back with a bowl of cold home-made compote, which we usually had to beg her to make. My eyes brightened and I felt that this had made my day. She filled a smaller bowl with the mixed fruit compote, put a teaspoon in it, and passed it to me.

I was happily surprised and dug into my bowl with great gusto and asked for a few more cherries and apricots. All the while I was telling her about school and my friend Sepideh, who had four sisters and they all live with her mother, but she never speaks of her father. Even though I can see the fun in being around all these little women, sometimes I cannot help but wonder how they cope without a father figure in the family.

"They have a townhouse with a big garden, and the sisters are so lively and helpful around the house, but I don't know how they manage without a father," I said with sympathy in my voice.

"Do you miss your father?" Meme suddenly asked. "Do you fear that he may not come back?"

I put down the spoon and began to cry, and no matter how much I tried I couldn't stop the tears. I felt lonely and didn't want to share my feelings with anyone in the family. *They must do enough thinking and worrying about him themselves*, I thought. Besides, what could they say but "He'll be fine, he will come back soon—you'll see!" I had heard it all before.

"It is difficult, I know," Meme comforted me. "I say that I know because it was my father who took care of us when my mother passed away. He used to travel from Yazd, where I was born and raised, to Tehran. You have every right to worry. I still remember looking out the window on the day he would leave on business until the day he was expected to return.

"I was three years old when my mother passed away, and I always feared losing my father too," she continued, reading my facial expression. "In those days it was much more difficult when phone communications were not as simple as today. I assume you speak to your father every evening before bed?"

I nodded. Then she kissed my forehead, sensing that I wanted to leave to finish my studies.

Two hours later, when I couldn't take in another word and couldn't care less about my exam, I gave it up and decided to join the others. To my surprise, I found my mother and grandmother had put out pillows, covers, and mattresses for all four of us in the TV room in front of the TV. It was like a dream come true. I had always wondered what it would look and feel like if we ever dared to attempt what they had done.

My father wouldn't allow many things. Eating in front of the television and sleeping in the TV room were against two of his rules—both of which we were about to break now. I must admit that the nuts and fruits we were eating, half-sitting on the mattresses in front of the TV, tasted even better.

"Tomorrow afternoon Dayee will be here to take us to their place so we can sleep over and come home on Friday evening and have a relaxing weekend," my mother said. (Friday is the weekend in Iran).

"This must be how it feels wanting to fly without wings," I said out loud excitedly. But then I changed my tone. "Does dad know?"

"Of course he does! He is going to call us there, but you have to behave so we can do this more often," my mother replied.

As I brushed my teeth later, I wondered if Ashkan knew and if he felt the same way we did.

"Anyway, tomorrow morning we are going to the shops—I have some shopping to do," my mother said to my grandmother as she was turning the lights off.

"Have I told you about the wise Bohlool being invited to a dinner party?" Maman bozorg asked us, then continued to tell us the story without waiting for a response.

> Once Bohlool was invited to a dinner party, and he decided to accept the invitation just to be polite. There were people at the party from all over the country, all with strong educational backgrounds and respectable jobs. They were all very well dressed and well spoken of, so the scholar Bohlool decided to mingle with the crowd, but unfortunately people kept confusing him with the servants. Even though he was well known and respectable amongst the people in the society, no one really recognised him. Bohlool took this at heart and decided to leave early. On the way home he reflected on what had happened and what he needed to do to make his point come across.
>
> Later that same week he found out where the next dinner party would be held, and accepted the invitation as soon as he received it. Days before the party he went clothes shopping and bought himself a satin robe in dark blue, trousers to go with it, and a nice white shirt in the best cotton available. Before leaving his house he put on his best turban with his best jewellery. Gold, diamonds, rubies, and pearls hung from his turban, neck and arms.
>
> As he came through the door he was warmly greeted and all the people in the room surrounded him, wanting his attention, asking questions and making flattering comments. Later he was shown into the dining room, where they put him at the head of the table as the guest of honour. When the food was served and people started to eat, he took a handful of the food on his plate and smeared it all over his clothes. From top to bottom he was covered in rice, vegetables, yoghurt, and grilled chicken and lamb.
>
> People looked at him with astonishment until the host dared to ask him about his behaviour. 'Now that I have your attention,' he said, 'allow me to explain myself. Earlier this week I was invited for dinner and I believe that majority of people I see here before me were invited to the same party. I wasn't recognised nor was I treated as a guest, but today

when I come here with my expensive clothes and jewellery, I am asked to be the guest of honour. Clearly the food, the respect, and the attention is for the clothes and not for me!

"We are still going shopping tomorrow," my mother said, clearly talking to my grandmother

5

I had been waiting for this moment all day, I thought as soon as I saw my amoo's car outside the school gate.

"Amani, your lift is here," the school guard shouted, then quickly realised that no announcement was necessary as I was already in car and ready to go.

"He has gotten used to the idea that someone other than your father is picking you up from school now," my amoo said, relieved that he didn't have to explain to the guard why he was picking me up or show the written permission slip from my mother. "How inconsiderate of me—how was your exam?"

"It was okay. I won't know for sure until I get the result back, and knowing Khanom Jallili, it probably will take a couple of weeks."

"Well, I heard that you are going to spend the weekend at your dayee's, which must be a nice way of celebrating," he said as he passed me the keys to the garage.

I opened the garage door and then ran upstairs to the second floor, and as I went to press the buzzer I noticed a different pair of shoes where Maman bozorg's shoes had been placed outside the door. Out of respect, she always placed her shoes outside the door. My heart started to bounce as I feared the worst.

Unfortunately, my fears were realised when I found my mum and her mother in the kitchen, debating shoes and feet. Maman bozorg looked a bit tired of the debate and was ready to surrender, and my mother was waiting for her to do so.

"You give it a try," my mother said, "you never know—you may even like them."

"I don't have a choice now, do I?! The shoes—*my* shoes that you have just put in the bin—had just adjusted themselves to my feet and just started to feel comfortable."

I felt for Maman bozorg and knew what a problem it was for her to find shoes that would fit her feet. Besides, she didn't like to throw out anything—not even worn-out shoes. I recognised myself in Maman bozorg. It took awhile for me to get used to something, and once I got used to something it was very difficult for me to detach myself from it.

The sound of my dayee's car came as a blessed saviour, and we all rushed to get our packed bags and jump into the car so that he didn't have to wait long. None of us really wanted to be stuck in the rush hour and lose more of our precious time together.

§ § § § §

There was nothing more satisfying than having Maman bozorg's *ghourmeh sabzi* (beef and herb stew) and *mourgh aloo* (chicken and plum stew) with saffron rice, and when I thought it couldn't get any better, she came out from the kitchen holding a fairly big bowl of home-made *torshi* (aubergine, onion, and tomato pickle).

Later that evening, after playing every game we could think of with Ashkan, we crashed in front of the television. It was then that he asked a question that turned all our heads around: "Can we sleep on the *bala-poshteboom* tonight?"—the rooftop.

We were *never* allowed to sleep on the rooftop, although I had heard that it was very cool and pleasant, especially when it had been a hot day, as it was today.

The *bala-poshteboom* was special to the urban Iranian household, as I understood it. It was a place for a lot of sleepovers during hot nights. Love stories created by communication with the girl or boy next door evolved there, as did arguments over the antennas between the inhabitants of the apartments. Children played hide and seek between the clothes that were hanging there to dry, and thieves sought to hide behind the air-conditioning units. Some kept pigeons in small cages up there to train as pets—and let's not forget the history that was made when the nation protested against Shah's regime by ranting Allah o Akbar from the rooftops.

"It's torture when the sun comes up early in the morning and blinds you," my dayee warned.

"We could wake up before the sunrise and come downstairs for either breakfast, or sleep down here for the rest of the morning," Shahin argued.

I knew that Dad would never allow us to do it, but I was hoping that my mum would agree to this. It was something that I'd always wanted to try.

I noticed that everyone was looking at my mum, as if they knew the ball was in her court. I was too frightened to say anything, in case my begging and pleading would make it worse, so I waited with anticipation while biting my upper lip.

"Rostam"—my father—"would never agree to it, but he is not here now and I don't mind, just this once," she said.

Overwhelmed with joy, we ran upstairs to have a look and to mark our territory with the mattresses, and in between we had a pillow fight over Maman bozorg's sleeping arrangements.

"I will sleep here," she said, interrupting the game. She made her bed in between the two empty ready-made beds. I raced Ashkan to one of the beds and got the one to the left of my grandmother's, then put my pillow down on the mattress on her right for Shahin. But I noticed that he was already fast asleep so I gave this one to Ashkan.

"Just the way I like it, with one Vazeer"—Minister—"on each side, my right and my left," my grandmother honoured us with a smile on her face.

"I don't want to be your left Vazeer!" I moaned.

"Why not?!"

"Do you even have to ask? In your stories, the left-side Vazeers are all nasty and mean to the core. The right-side Vazeers are always helpful and clever in a good way."

"Ashkan, why don't you change sides with Shirin?"

"Never—she was the one who offered this side to me, and when it's offered it can not be taken back."

"Yes, it can," I argued.

"Says who?"

"Says me!"

"Right, that's it," my grandmother said. Then she stood up, grabbed her pillow, and went to make her bed next to my mother.

"Look what you did!" I said, annoyed.

"Me? You really are something, you know that?"

"Maman bozorg, we are really sorry—please come back and we promise to behave," I pleaded. "We have been looking forward to hearing one of your stories tonight. This is the best part of the day." I continued to plead until she came back.

"I don't want to hear any more from either of you. From now on it is me who does the talking," she instructed us.

As we lay down, I felt a bit chilly, so I pulled the cover on me. It was early autumn, and there was a chance that it might get even chillier.

> *Yeki bood, yeki nabood*—there was once a king who was happily married and lived in a castle with his beautiful wife.
>
> One morning when the king was combing his hair in front the mirror he noticed a grey hair on his forehead. He was shocked and annoyed at the same time, so he plucked the hair and stormed into the queen's bedroom, despite the maid's protests.
>
> 'Look at this! I am growing old and I don't have any children yet,' he protested. 'I may be a childless king, but I am not going to die as one. I am giving you until the end of the month to break the news of your pregnancy to me.'

The king stormed out in a rush and left the queen and the maid looking at each other with astonishment.

'What am I to do?' the queen cried as she knelt beside the bed and burst into tears.

'Ma'am should not give up hope like that. It is not good for your health to be worrying. I know someone Ma'am can see. She is a white witch and she has a reputation for helping people in need. We will smuggle Ma'am out of the palace this evening dressed as me so that Ma'am can see her tonight and ask for her advice. We must not waste any time!'

The queen, who was still shocked over the whole scenario, mumbled something like 'I don't understand how life can turn in a matter of minutes. How is that possible?'

Later that evening the queen managed to dress as the maid and sneak out of the palace and find her way to the white witch's place, after getting lost a couple of times—even though she had gone over the directions with the maid at the palace a few times. She knocked on the door the way she was directed to do so.

The witch took the knock as a sign of a familiar friend and opened the door. 'Who are you?' she asked as soon as she saw the queen standing in the doorway.

'Let me in, please. My maid sent me to you because I desperately need your help and you are the only one who can help me.' The queen started to tell her the story and sobbed, realising how desperate it all sounded.

Without saying a word, the witch looked under the sink in one of the cupboards and found a big red juicy apple. 'I knew I had it here somewhere,' she said. She held the apple in front of her face, locked her eyes on it, mumbled some words, and blew on it.

'You take this apple home with you, and before you share your bed with your husband tonight, have half of the apple yourself and offer the other half to him. You will break the news of the pregnancy not only to him but to the whole world in a month's time.'

The queen took the apple and had a closer look at this magic apple, which looked the same as any apple, and thought that no one would guess its magic powers unless they were told about it. In her moment of joy she kissed the apple and as she was about to express her thanks, the witch spoke: 'You'd better listen because there is a catch. After the nine months you will give birth to a healthy and beautiful baby boy. The whole world will admire the child and you will be appreciated for given the king an heir. The catch is not to put the child on the ground until he is one year old.'

The queen was happy and overjoyed. She took the apple and thanked the witch, and promised to show her appreciation in gold by morning. She rushed home before people at the palace noticed her absence.

'Remember to have half of the apple each tonight and not to put the child down on the ground for a year…' the witch shouted as she watched the queen disappear into the woods.

As the queen was trying to find her way back in the dark, she couldn't stop wondering what would happen if she would put the child down before he reached one year of age. She decided not to think about that, but to focus instead on the apple and her plans to seduce the king. As she took a deep breath, she entered the dining room with a big, seductive smile and her head held up, prepared to have dinner with the king.

Nine months, nine days, and nine hours later the country cheered and celebrated as the news about the new-born heir to the king was spread. The king was overjoyed when he finally held his son in his arms.

'He reminds me of my father,' said the king. 'I will name him Arshan'—hero. 'Yes, he is an Arshan and we will throw a party a year from now to celebrate a naming ceremony for the future king.'

The queen worried about the child's safety and hardly allowed anyone to touch Arshan, and knew that she wasn't able to really enjoy the birth of her son fully as she constantly worried for his safety.

She was still wondering about the consequences of putting the child on the ground, but she couldn't afford to risk it. She counted the days and the months and couldn't wait to celebrate her son's birthday. She was constantly tired as she hadn't had a proper night's sleep and didn't feel that she could trust anyone with her child.

Like anyone with a difficult period in their life that seems it would never end, but eventually does, the queen woke up one day and to her relief had to plan for her son's birthday party for the following week.

It took a lot of planning and shopping. There would be entertainment, and people from all over the world would be invited. The best spices, rice, and cotton for tablecloths from India, the best silk and satin for the royal outfits from China, the best diamonds for the royal jewellery from southern Africa, the best herbs and smelly oil from mid-Africa and stones such as jade from northern Africa were ordered.

A lot of preparations were also made back home in honour of the prince. There were hand-woven carpets in silk made with the young prince's face on them in his honour. Everyone was busy right up until the day before the celebration.

Finally the day was about to arrive, and everyone—the people and the Royals alike—celebrated, cheered, ate, drank, sang, and danced. There had been not such celebrations in the land since the prince was crowned.

The king had been waiting for this day for a long time and generously shared his feelings of joy and happiness with his nation. The queen's feelings were divided between joy and impatience. She just wanted her son to reach his first year of age. She was tired of worrying about anyone putting him on the ground. Not many people had touched the prince, let alone held him for that reason.

A few minutes before midnight, as the queen held the prince in her arms, the king summoned her to greet the public with him. He asked her to wave to the people with him, so she handed the child to his nanny, who was sitting next to them. The queen left the prince in her arms and whispered to her not to put the child on the ground. Feeling confident, she held the king by his waist and waved to the nation with pride as the city clock rang twelve times. Finally the queen breathed a sigh of relief and turned around to retrieve her son so she could hold him in her own arms and kiss him on his first birthday.

The queen looked with astonishment when she saw the nanny looking for something, as if she had lost something. There was no sign of the prince. The queen, struggling to breathe, rushed over to look for her son.

'I can't find him, Ma'am,' cried the nanny. 'I just put him down here and he is gone. I don't know where he went.'

'Why did you put him down?' she screamed. 'I told you specifically not to.'

'I thought Ma'am told me to put him on the ground, Ma'am. I…'

'You fool! Why would I tell you to do that? You tell me exactly what happened.'

'I put him here on this spot and he just disappeared. I have looked everywhere for him but no one has seen him.'

The queen tried to hide her shock as she noticed that she had drawn attention to herself. She gathered herself, smiled to the crowd and realised that she had to act quickly.

As soon as she found a free moment and felt that the party was continuing without any help from her and that her absence would not be noticed, she jumped on a horse and rode as fast as she could in dark towards the white witch's cabin.

She soon found the cabin and, out of breath, knocked on the door. After a moment of hesitation, she walked in.

'I was expecting you,' she heard the witch say, but she could not see her.

'Tell me where my son is. Tell me what you have done with him,' she cried out.

'Your son is beyond my abilities now. I gave you a son and clear instructions about how to keep him, but you ignored them.'

'I do not have time to explain or to be lectured,' the queen thought, then, with a harsh voice, she said, 'Help me get my son back or God help you.'

'This is no time for threats and unfriendliness,' replied the witch. 'It is beyond my knowledge to locate your son. It is out of my hands, now. I am sorry.'

The queen sank to the floor. She didn't want to think about the loss of her one-year-old son, the loss of her position as a queen, and possibly her own death by hanging tomorrow at dawn as soon as the king heard about the disappearance of his heir. 'I can not allow this to happen,' she said and rose. I am going to find my son. I will leave in darkness so no one will notice.'

'Prepare to lose your life on this journey,' the witch warned.

'Don't you understand? I am already dead either way. I might as well die looking for my son.'

'Well, you do have a point. Listen carefully. I do not know where you son is, but I know a little about the journey. I will tell you as much as I know to prepare you.'

'First and foremost, you cannot allow anyone to know that you are a woman. These journeys are not for women. Secondly, follow your intuition and the signs given to you. All the signs are valid and do not lie. Listen to the animals—their instincts are to be trusted. Thirdly, you will be entering a world that has not interested you before. You have to learn to trust your love for your son. It is only then that you will do whatever it will take to bring him back.

'Last but not least, you will need this pack.' The queen unwrapped some tissue and saw a needle, a pinch of salt, and a piece of raw meat. 'You will know when you have to use it for aid.'

'Why did you not tell me this before when I was devastated and asked you to help me?'

'Because I had to make sure that you really wanted your son back.' As the queen reached for the door handle, the witch continued: 'And also because no woman that I have helped so far has come back to tell me about their journey.'

"The rest of the story continues tomorrow," Maman bozorg said suddenly, interrupting the story.

"What? Huh? Ashkan and I protested. "That was not our deal," I said.

"There was no deal to begin with," Maman bozorg said.

"But…we can't wait until tomorrow night. We will not have this opportunity tomorrow to listen to the story together. Tomorrow is Friday and we have to go back in the afternoon because school starts on Saturday," we pleaded.

"But you are both falling asleep. I can hear it in your heavy breathing. You don't want to miss a part of the story, do you?"

"We are not falling asleep! How can we? It has only become interesting," said Ashkan.

"Maman bozorg! Please?" I tried.

"Ammeh?"—Auntie—Ashkan pleaded with my mum for support. My mother was Ashkan's father's sister.

"Don't involve me!" my mother said. "Maman bozorg is tired and has a dry throat. Can you not hear that in her voice?"

"I am sorry, Maman bozorg," I said, and handed her a glass of water that my mum always places with us so that we don't have to ask for water over and over again during the night. "Have a sip—you will feel better soon."

After a smile and a sip of water, she was convinced and continued.

> The queen remembered her promise to not reveal her gender. She dressed like a man and cut her hair with a knife, and was ready to ride into the dark again. She wanted to explain everything to someone, or at least to say goodbye to her maid, but she did not dare for her safety as well as her own.
>
> She tied the package to her saddle without having a clue where to start or where to ride to. Instead she trusted her horse to choose a direction.
>
> She rode and rode until she fell asleep on her horse. The horse had stopped for some water and when the queen opened her eyes the sun was up. She clapped her horse and chose a spot by the tree to allow the horse to drink from the lake and have a rest.
>
> She opened the package and saw the salt and the raw meat and the needle. She wondered what they were for—surely not for eating when she became hungry. The witch couldn't have been concerned about the queen's eating habits. From what the witch had said, there were other issues that she had to be concerned about, not hunger.

She decided to pick an apple from the tree to ease her hunger. As she took the first bite, she heard a very weak female voice, almost a whisper. She hid herself under the tree and listened carefully. 'But why, Sister? Why has she chosen to go on this journey?'

'You would do anything for your child,' said a second faint voice.

'What does she have to do?'

'She has to follow the *lohes.*'—directions, warnings, and signs written on stones. 'They would lead her to the Deeve.'

'Who is the Deeve?'

'What is the Deeve?' would be the question. 'The prince is captured by the two-horned giant.'

'Have you seen him?'

'No, Sister! No one has seen the Deeve. Those who have haven't returned to tell us about him.'

'This may be the last time we see the queen, then.'

'Perhaps, Sister, perhaps.'

'You are saying that no one has been or is able to defeat the Deeve?'

'Well, there is one way. One needs to find his *Shisheye Omr.*'

'What is that?'

'I have heard that people fight him as soon as they find him. Sometimes it is about skill and not about brute force. In this case you need to be clever enough to find the bottle that contains his life, and his life will come to an end as soon as you break that bottle. That is the only way to defeat the Deeve. All it takes is wisdom, which is the only thing the Deeve is lacking.'

'I truly hope that the queen can find the Deeve's *Shisheye Omr* and break it.'

'I hope so too. She would not only save her son but also so many others who have been his prisoners for many, many years. His castle is full of children he has stolen, and also the parents he has captured who have come for them.'

With that the two sisters agreed between themselves to leave, and for the first time the queen was able to catch a glimpse of them. She was amazed to see that the sisters were two beautiful white birds with golden stripes on their wings.

Magical sister birds that talk, *lohes,* a giant with two horns called a Deeve, whose life is in a bottle. Never in her life did she imagine that one day she would believe such things. She truly felt that she had entered a world beyond imagination.

She whistled for her horse, jumped on it, and whispered in his ear to take her to the Deeve.

They rode into the woods and the queen became aware as the horse gradually slowed down and eventually stopped. She looked around without knowing what she was looking for until she found an unusual stone with some scripts on it. She came off her horse and took a closer look and whispered to herself:

'This must be the *lohe*,' she thought. 'This must be it.' It said, 'You are about to enter the darkest world you can imagine. Turn around if you are not ready to face the evil. Turn around if you have slightest fear or doubt.'

The queen thought, "How can I be frightened of the things that I have not seen or know about? How can I have doubts about saving my child from the evil giant? How can I turn my back to that?' She had never felt any surer about anything else in her life. She carried on until she came to a crossing. She stood there not knowing which way to go until she saw a second *lohe*. 'If you want to turn back, take the left road, which will lead you to the next city, but if you want to continue this journey, take the right road and it will take you to the Deeve's castle,' it said.

The queen led her horse to the right, but the horse refused. She looked at the animal and saw the fear in its eyes. The queen decided to leave him there and whispered in his ear, 'On the third day I will meet you here. You wait for me and the prince—but remember to leave on the fourth day.'

She chose her path and continued with grace and determination. After awhile she could see the castle from afar, and the nearer she got to the castle, the more fascinated she became.

It was the biggest castle she had ever seen, and the sunset was making it even more beautiful, setting down behind it, the castle turning from yellow to orange and from orange to red, and then suddenly purple by the time she reached the gate, which no one seemed to be watching. After studying the surroundings long and hard, she decided to enter the castle without permission.

As soon as she fell on the other side of the gate, she saw a girl standing above her. 'Come quick,' she said. 'Come on, he is about to wake up. Come!'

'Who are you?' the queen asked.

'I am his most recent prisoner. I knew that it wouldn't take long before someone would come for their child.'

'Have seen my baby? Have you seen my child?' asked the queen.

'Have I seen him?! I feed him, change him, and nurture him every day. He is a lovely boy. There will be time enough later to tell you more; right now I have to hide you. The Deeve has an incredible sense of smell and may find you very quickly.'

The queen wiped her tears and followed the girl, not knowing whether she was to be trusted or not. She felt she had no other choice.

The girl took her to the back of the kitchen and hid her behind sacks of rice, potatoes, and onions in the storage room. Suddenly the castle shook to a sound as loud as an earthquake—a sound that made them both shake to the core.

'He is awake,' the girl cried. 'Quick! Change your clothes with me. There is no time—I will explain later. Trust me!'

The queen only managed to take off her blouse and exchange it with the girl. There was no time for the rest—they could hear the Deeve getting closer and closer.

'Do not allow your curiosity to cost you your life,' the girl said and shoved her back amongst the sacks.

'Where is my dinner?' she heard the Deeve shout. He had the loudest voice she had ever heard. The king was also loud, and when he yelled the cities around would be aware of his anger, but the Deeve was louder. She was curious, but remembered the girl's warning.

Instead she just remained hidden and listened. It sounded as if the girl had brought him his dinner and he'd finished within minutes.

'There is smell of fresh meat in the house,' he yelled. She could hear him wander around the kitchen and open the storage room door. She could hear the sound of her own knees knocking against each other.

'I have worn the blouse that I wore the first time you saw me,' the queen heard the girl say. 'Do you remember? Perhaps that is what smells so fresh to you.'

The Deeve looked at the girl with confusion. 'Come here,' he said. 'It cannot be your smell.'

'It has changed since I entered your castle. But this is how I smelled in the beginning.' she explained calmly.

The girl's bravery gave the queen energy, and she calmed down a little.

The Deeve said with great confusion, 'Yes—what else? No idiot would enter the castle willingly.'

After dinner, the girl played sitar, sang, and danced for him all night. Unable to stay awake, the queen dozed off behind all the sacks.

She woke with a start when she heard the girl moving towards to the sacks. 'He has finally fallen asleep. We have to hurry, we have so little time.'

'Can I see my son?' was the first thing the queen asked.

'We will have enough time for that later. Believe me—he is still fine, but right now we need to focus on how to free him and ourselves. Otherwise we will be stuck here forever.'

'I heard that he has a *Shisheye Omr*. He can only be destroyed by destroying the bottle.'

'Yes! You have been taught well.'

'But I do not know where it is. Do you?'

'That is a long story. The *Shisheye Omr* is in a box that is locked, and the key to the box has been fed to the fish in the pond in the middle of the garden and watched over by a bird most loyal to Deeve, who reports to the Deeve by singing as soon as someone gets near it.

'People have tried to free their loved ones by using force to open the box, thinking that it would be impossible to get the key. Some even thought to use force to kill the Deeve, but the Deeve recovers quickly from knife wounds wherever he is stabbed. Some tried to escape and had no luck. There are so many that are locked away here in the castle.'

'How come you are as free as you are in castle?'

The girl smiled at the queen's suspiciousness, but understood where she was coming from and therefore explained patiently: 'This is where women start when they are first captured. I will soon be replaced by someone else. That is why we have so little time. My time should run out in a couple of days.'

The queen remembered that she had told her horse to wait for three days and then leave if she was not back by then. She had to trust the girl—she had no choice.

The queen sat down to think of a plan. It seemed impossible to think of a solution. Everything that she could think had already been tried. But then again, she remembered the birds and the white witch's advice: 'Wisdom is all that is needed.'

'Have you ever seen the bird leaving its nest? Have you heard it being distracted?' the queen asked, as if she had a plan in mind. She continued when she saw the girl shaking her head in response. 'Listen carefully and remember it well. This evening you need to find out from the Deeve what makes the bird so loyal to him.'

'This evening? We do not have enough time!'

'We have to do this properly! People who are imprisoned in the castle have been trying to destroy him by force. They've lacked patience or rational thinking. We need to learn from that.'

'Tell me what to do!'

'You need to feed him with hearty food and good wine this evening. When you have gained his trust and he is drunk enough, ask him about the bird. I trust you to know the Deeve well enough to know how to approach him about that.

'Then we need to know about the box and where it is hidden. Even if we could get the key, there would not be enough time for us start searching the whole castle.'

'That I know! I found it by accident when I had first arrived. Besides, it wasn't very well hidden. The Deeve believes in guarding the key rather than the box.'

The evening approached sooner than they wanted. The girl, with the queen's help, planned a feast for the Deeve. The aroma of food carried for miles. Good wine was ready to be served and the table was set—a meal fit for royalty. The queen felt confident about her plan, and deep down felt that the girl was clever enough to pull it off.

She hid where she had hidden the night before and waited patiently for the Deeve to stomp his way through to the kitchen and ask for food. She felt the ground and the walls shake as the Deeve got closer and closer.

'There is that smell again!" he yelled out.

'Good sense of smell you have," said the girl. 'I have roasted a fresh lamb, slaughtered only this morning in your honour.'

'It is the smell of fresh human flesh,' the Deeve said.

'I have also made you saffron rice, aubergine yoghurt, and fresh stone baked bread.' The queen could feel herself getting hungry as the girl talked about the food.

The girl brought out the food dish by dish, and as she turned to carve the lamb, half was gone, and only a leg was sticking out of the Deeve's enormous mouth. The picture frightened the girl even more and felt that soon it could be her leg sticking out of his mouth, if that was his wish.

Finally she brought out the wine and filled his glass, then refilled it as soon as the Deeve had drunk it.

After finishing the third bottle of wine and reaching for a fourth, the girl started to sing his favourite song. It seemed that he was enjoying himself as he was humming along while eating and drinking more.

'You have a good voice,' the Deeve said.

The girl smiled. 'The bird in the garden also has a good voice. It is a shame that she only sings when she wants to.'

'She sings to warn me,' the Deeve said.

'I have never seen her fly, eat or leave her spot.'

'She is fed by me,' the Deeve said. 'Her eating habits are unusual. I need to feed her special meat that has been buried and matured under ground for years and years.'

'It must be difficult to feed her every day,' said the girl. "Perhaps I can help you with that?'

'No need! Besides, I only feed her once a month. That is the only time she is distracted from her watch. It takes a while for her to process the food, but then I keep watch while she eats.' The Deeve paused, then said, 'Enough about the bird. Sing to me!'

The girl filled his glass while singing and sang another song, and then several after that, until the Deeve allowed her to rest her voice. 'I have had many girls come and go, and you will be replaced soon, but I want you to know that you have been my favourite so far.' And on that note he passed out on the dining table.

The queen didn't dare to move until the girl whispered to her in the storeroom that it was safe to leave. She'd had some time to think of a plan while the girl had been working hard to put the Deeve to sleep.

When the Deeve had mentioned the special meat for the bird, she remembered the pack that the white witch had given her on her last visit. She looked for the pack in her pockets and opened it. There it was—the matured, ill-smelling, almost black meat.

On the way to the garden, the queen told the girl about her plan to have her distract the bird by feeding it the special meat that she had with her. Meanwhile, she would try to catch the fish in the pond for the key to the box.

With the meat in her hand, the girl vanished into the darkness near the tree where the bird nested. The queen was unsure of how to catch the fish—it was easier said than done. She knew it could take hours for her to try with her bare hands.

She thought that perhaps she could empty the pond, but how would she do that? That would also take hours. She didn't have enough time for that either, and she imagined the bird had started its meal by now.

'I must be missing something,' she whispered to herself. 'I must be overlooking something. It must be right before my eyes.' She closed her eyes and emptied her thoughts, and asked the universe for guidance. Suddenly it dawned on her. 'The pack!'

She opened it and poured the salt into the water. It didn't take very long before the fish was floating on the top of the water. She took the fish and opened its mouth—and there it was, the golden key shining behind its teeth.

With the key in her hand, she whispered to the girl, and they made their way to the castle.

'How did you manage that?' the girl asked, feeling proud to have been a part the mission they had accomplished. 'I have heard about so many men and women trying to find the key, without success.'

'With help from friends like you. But we still have a long way. Show me to the box,' the queen said.

They entered the castle. The Deeve's loud snoring assured them they were safe. The girl entered a hallway that lead them to a room with a royal chair covered by a silk Persian rug—the most beautiful rug, the queen had ever seen. Under the rug sat the box!

The queen uncovered the box, gently put the key inside the lock, opened it, and lifted the top. There rested the shining glass bottle. 'It is amazing that the life of such a powerful Deeve lies in a glass bottle that can easily break into pieces. So powerful, yet so fragile, don't you think?' she asked the girl.

'Have you noticed that this room is covered with carpets?' the girl said. 'We will have difficulty breaking the bottle here.'

The queen looked around, took the bottle out of the box, and ran out to the hallway. To her amazement, the hallway was also covered by thick carpets. She tried to open a window, but they all seemed locked.

The queen started to panic when she realised that she no longer could hear the Deeve's snoring. It seemed that the glass bottle was protected against breaking by the cushioned castle. She was about to leave through the glass door to the garden when suddenly all the doors shut.

'It is my life you are carelessly holding in your hands, my dear,' she heard the Deeve say.

She was too frightened to look behind her. She was too frightened to look forward. She wanted to shut her eyes and disappear, as her son had days ago.

'You have played it very well so far—I have to give you that,' he said. 'I cannot remember ever seeing anyone holding my *Shisheye Omr* in their hands.'

All the queen could think about was how to break the bottle and relieve everyone of their misery. Until she finished her job, she would accomplish nothing.

She knew that there were only moments before either she or the Deeve died. She had to take a chance. She closed her eyes and thought of her son, and with a strength from desperation, anger, and frustration; she hurled the bottle against one of the windows.

'Noooo...!' the Deeve screamed, his voice fading. Finally she dared to open her eyes. The *Shisheye Omr* had broken through the window and broken into pieces on the garden pavement. The Deeve, meanwhile, had become a huge pile of black dust. The girl was standing at the top of the stairs, looking on with astonishment.

'Show me to my son,' the queen demanded. 'We have so little time!' She thought of her horse, which had been ordered to leave by dawn.

They went through the castle and opened the doors with force, and in each room they found mothers, fathers, and children who had been captured and imprisoned over the years.

The queen didn't have time to empathise with prisoners as she moved quickly from room to room. She just had to find her son as soon as possible. And finally, when she opened the door to the last room on that floor, she saw a golden cage in the centre, and in it was the prince, sitting quietly and trying to entertain himself by making sounds with his fingers against the bars.

The queen knelt down next to the cage and tried to catch his attention. She was crying silently, sad tears for losing him a few nights ago and happy ones for finding him, relieved that he was alive. She could not begin to imagine what plans the Deeve had for the little prince.

She slid her hand through the bars and gave him time to familiarise himself with her voice and hand. When he was ready, he stroked her hand and held onto it. With her other hand, she studied the lock on the cage and noticed that it was no ordinary lock. She sighed. She thought she'd have to remove the whole cage and take it with her, but she found that it would not move—it was attached to the floor.

She sat down, took a deep breath, and once again asked for wisdom. She closed her eyes and felt that there had to be a way.

'The needle!' she shouted. "I have a needle left in my pack, which I have not used. It is worth a try. After all, the contents of the pack were supposed to be used on this journey.' With that, she put the needle inside the lock and turned and twisted a couple of times until she heard a click. She opened the cage and held out her hands for the prince. He hesitated at first, then reached to wipe the tears off his mother's face. Then he crawled forward and left the cage.

She called for the girl and headed towards the gate, where a crowd of people were leaving the castle. 'You saved them all,' the girl said.

'Remember—I had a lot of help from you, and other good friends.'

The queen looked to see if the horse was still at the crossing where she had left it. The horse saw her first, and in his own way of greeting, he offered all three of them a ride with pleasure.

They rode towards the light, and soon the sun appeared. Not long after they could see the castle, and soon after that they reached the gate. The king was notified, and the Royals joined them and cheered in joy.

The king, queen, and prince lived happily ever after, and the girl joined the royal family as the queen's loyal friend and companion. They had promised not to tell anyone about their unique experience and journey. After all, who would have believed them? Talking sister birds, *lohes*, a Deeve, a *Shish-eye Omr*, a meat-eating bird, and a magic needle!

The queen was sure that she wanted to keep the story to herself, and was happy to have someone to share it with when necessary. "As for the white witch, she was invited annually to attend and to celebrate the prince's birthday, and each year she declined.

People who had been freed from the Deeve's castle joined their families and friends in their hometowns and lived to tell their children and grandchildren of the brave woman who had saved them from evil.

"This is without a doubt one of my favourite stories," I said. "Each time you tell it, it is as if you read from a book. You don't miss a word. You amaze me, Maman bozorg. I love you!"

"For my favourite, I have difficulty choosing between this one and the wise prince who travels to find himself and learn about life," Ashkan said.

"You only say that because the main character in that story is a male," I complained.

"And this is your favourite story because the hero is a female."

"This is my favourite story because it portrays reality—heroism and wisdom in a female as it is. But put that aside. It is a story of the love of a mother for her child."

"How do you know if the queen did what she did out of love for the child and not out of love for herself? We know that the king would have killed her if she had not gone after her baby."

"Men! What would you know about a love of a mother for her child?"

"As much as you would!" Ashkan argued.

"At least I will be a mother one day."

"Perhaps on that day you will learn what motherly love really means, but until then you know as little as I do."

"The arrogant king who ordered the queen to get pregnant, the queen who is questioned, even today, whether she risked her life for her own safety or for her child's, and the fact that she could not reveal that she was a female in order to protect men's dignity—or even take credit for what she had achieved. As much as times have changed since then, I certainly do not see any major changes," I said, perhaps wanting to open the door to a whole new argument.

"Of course times have changed…"

"Enough!" Maman bozorg ordered. "I want to sleep. Look at Shahin. Why can you not behave more like him?"

We both turned our heads to look at Shahin—who had fallen asleep before the story had even begun.

"We didn't want to miss the story. Besides, how appreciative would we be of you if we fell asleep in the middle of the story?" Ashkan and I said together.

"Isn't that the purpose of the stories—to put children to sleep—during them or at least afterwards?"

"Not your stories! Those boring ones like Cinderella, Snow White, or the three pigs and a wolf, and…"

"Enough! Goodnight."

We knew that she meant it. I looked at the sky. So many stars! It was so beautiful. I felt that I was lost in the sky amongst the stars. I had never felt as close to the stars until that moment. I cherished every moment, as if it would be the last time that I would ever experience such closeness to the stars on Maman bozorg's rooftop, with the people I loved more than life in the land of Persia.

And as it turned out, it was.

6

"Don't put your head out of the window like a dog," my mother said.

"What about like a girl who needs some fresh air?"

Mother sighed. "There is no fresh air in Tehran these days. It is pollution you are breathing in."

On that note, a discussion started amongst the others in the car, about how it was then and how it is now, and the way things were going to be.

I quit reviewing my day in silence and ignored the sadness that surrounded the city on Friday afternoons. I could not believe that it had only been twelve hours since we had woken up to Maman bozorg's famous delicious breakfast. That was the best part of Friday mornings. For those who preferred a hot breakfast; she fried eggs with a touch of fresh *Kermani* cumin seeds on top, accompanied by *halim*—a famous Iranian porridge made with oats and turkey and topped with melted butter and cinnamon, with freshly baked *barbary* (Iranian bread) on the side.

For those who liked a cold breakfast, she would cut tomatoes with cucumbers and feta cheese, and for those who had a sweet tooth; she prepared a bowl of her home-made sweet-and-sour cherry jam, accompanied by honey, butter, and cream.

I loved to wake up to the smell of breakfast at Maman bozorg's. I would normally have a little bit of everything, wash it down with samovar-brewed tea, and not give up until I was so full that I could barely move. She smiled to see us so happy, gathered around her, eating, laughing, and making jokes.

At the traffic light, I saw a child who was crying and complaining that the weekend was too short and refusing to say goodbye to her grandparents.

That was the story of Friday afternoons. All week the adults worked long days and hours, children went to school and worked hard on their heavy course loads, and all looked forward to Thursday afternoon and Friday—the Iranian weekend. Extended families would get together and have Friday lunches. Come Friday afternoon, the city became dead and the souls equally silent.

I considered myself lucky because we had made the most of Thursday evening and most of Friday this week, until we truly had to leave to prepare ourselves for the week ahead.

"So it is settled then—you will bring Ashkan Jaan over on Wednesday afternoon," I heard my mum say.

Wednesday afternoon? I thought. *I cannot be hearing this right. What about school on Thursday?* I didn't dare to question it, though, in case by chance they had forgotten about school, and I didn't want to be corrected in case I had not heard correctly. I wanted to live in the moment, thinking that we would have an extra day of weekend.

When we were finally about to say our goodbyes, I held my breath for a moment, prepared to either be disappointed or scream with joy.

The Iranian way of saying goodbye is a very painful one. You start by thanking each other for one's hospitality, kindness, and generosity, then you apologise for the trouble and the bother you have caused during the time you spent with each other, then you express your sadness for having to say goodbye. Last but not least—the moment that I had been waiting for—you start planning the next visit. That was when I heard them mention Wednesday afternoon again.

I could not believe my ears. I ran upstairs, and only when I looked in the diary did I remember that the holy Islamic day—a national holiday—would fall on this Thursday. Usually when we have a longer weekend we seize the opportunity and drive to Caspian Sea, which is only a four-hour drive. It can get very crowded on the way there and back, but it was worth the hassle, just to be spending time in the fresh air and the sea breeze, even if only for a couple of days.

Last time we went was two months ago, when we enjoyed the three weeks of summer break in the family villa. Usually as many of us as possible would go so we could all enjoy ourselves. This is the Iranian way of travelling—"The more the merrier," is the motto. The extended family—aunts and uncles with their children and grandchildren—all travel and spend as much quality time together as possible to get away from the hectic life of Tehran.

Last time we had planned the trip well ahead, and anyone able to join was welcome. A minibus with a driver was hired to drive fifteen of us to the villa in Ramsar. In the group there were five children and ten adults, only two of the adults were men. One was my amoo, my Father's brother, and the other was my father's dayee, who was retired and could be away for three weeks.

During those three weeks we had a daily cleaning and cooking schedule, with two adults handling these chores at a time while the rest had the freedom to do as they wished during the day, with a lovely home-made dinner to come home to. It was up to each how they wanted to team up. We children were exempt from the chores, but when our mothers or guardians were on their shifts, we could not leave the villa and were restricted as to where we could play.

My mum's best friend, who was my dad's cousin, had come with us, and I could tell how my mother had been looking forward to be on a holiday with her friend. Khaleh (auntie) Shokouh loved Mum equally, and they enjoyed each other's company. They had so much to talk and laugh about that I almost thought it was childish. Their common theme was to be playful and childlike and not to be embarrassed about it. I never understood the bond between them—or perhaps I felt too envious of the relationship to understand it.

"Well, we know Shahla and Shokouh are a team, but what about the rest of us?" my father's dayee Seerous said when they were pairing up.

When off duty, we had the whole day to go to the seaside, bathe, play in the sand building sand castles, pick figs, and laugh and sing all the way back to the villa. Or we could go sightseeing in the beautiful city of Ramsar. In the middle of the city there was one of the Shah's former summer villas, now open to the public. It had a beautiful garden and a room full of activities and games for the children.

Some days were wasted on shopping for souvenirs that, from experience, we knew we would have no use for as soon as we returned to Tehran. Only the sweets, jam, and pastries—*kolocheh*, for instance—would be a sweet reminder of the trip while sipping tea back home.

We quickly learned that we wouldn't look forward to meals every time we returned to the villa. After tasting each pair's cooking, we just about decided that some evenings we could do without dinner. Some made traditional dishes so traditional that they would taste unusual. Others cooked with as little fat, salt, and spice as possible, the goal being healthy—and tasteless— dishes. Others made their dishes so bland and boring that you wanted to shout for some ketchup—which, of course, would have been very rude.

I enjoyed food and could be fussy when it came to eating and cooking. That's why I loved my mum's cooking, and the best evenings were when Mum and Khaleh Shokouh cooked.

After dinner, everyone gathered around to tell stories and jokes, play backgammon, and do tricks. We often asked my mum to sing. She would happily agree to do that—she had a lovely singing voice, and she knew it. It is customary to decline a couple of times when you are invited to sing or dance, and then to ask the others to accompany you. She, of course, politely followed the custom, but as soon everyone began the others would let Mum have the spotlight and sing out so that her voice filled the room with pleasure and joy. She usually asked everyone to join in and take part, and soon the room would be filled with disorganised tunes and noises—but also with love and laughter.

My dad called every evening around eleven, and my parents would be on the phone like a couple of lovebirds for over an hour sometimes. I, meanwhile, would fall asleep, and when I woke up to have some water, I could hear my mum and Khaleh Shokouh whispering until the early hours of the morning. They had stories to tell about themselves, the people around them, neighbours, families, husbands, and children.

Mum had the most beautiful big green eyes, which entitled her to her name—Shahla, "The one with the beautiful eyes." She also had a petite nose and lovely skin, and she always kept her hair short, with the kind of highlights that had recently become fashionable.

She was adored by everyone. She was kind, generous, and understanding. Meme always said that although she didn't have a daughter of her own, she had gained one because my dad had married my mum. My mum glowed in the glory of being so loved. I looked at my beautiful mum proudly in social gatherings, and wished that one day I could be as beautiful as her and have her skills of sewing, cooking, debating, and singing.

On a day when we went back to the villa from Ramsar, as soon as we reached the resort and passed the day-watch guards at the entrance, Khaleh Shokouh asked my mum to sing a song. She said that it would make the walk to the villa more pleasant. Mum agreed and started to sing softly, almost whispering, but soon her big soprano voice filled the air and Khaleh Shokouh joined in. A car stopped, and at first we assumed that they were guards warning us about the singing, but they were just a couple of young people enjoying the music and offering their voices and encouragement.

Suddenly Ms. Mary, who had apparently been watching the whole scene over the fence from her garden, asked us to join her for afternoon tea. Khale Shokouh and my mum looked at each other, almost as if they were seeking each other's approval. Ms. Mary was English and had been living in Ramsar for as long as we could remember, but we had never been invited to her villa. English afternoon tea sounded exciting, and I looked at Mum, hoping she would accept the invitation.

The adults had a moment of *tarof*, then finally accepted the invitation. "*Tarof*" means that you are not supposed to accept such invitations to dinner, food, sweets, and so on, the very first time. It goes back and forth a couple of times before someone finally gives in. Sometimes it can get boring or even irritating, but it was still a custom amongst Iranians in Iran—and even amongst those who were born abroad but brought up in an Iranian home.

Ms. Mary, however, was an English lady who had been living in Iran for a long time, and luckily she understood the custom and played the game before we finally entered her villa. It was as if I was entering England for the first time, as excited as I was. She had the most beautiful garden that I had ever seen. She had the most amazing roses, and many other flowers that I had never seen. She also had a couple of fruit trees, and she proudly and kindly asked if we'd like to taste some of the fruit. The tea was brought out by her loyal servant, and I was sitting impatiently to see what the fuss was about. The tea, Earl Grey, was served in the most beautiful china cups, and had a heavenly scent. The shortbread was so buttery and nice that I forgot my manners and helped myself to two. The scones, cream, and jam all went amazingly well together. I couldn't contain my excitement and felt so happy that I asked if I could have a closer look at some of the roses. I stood amongst them in the middle of the garden and breathed in their fresh and beautiful smell—a real English rose garden!

We all felt energised by the experience, and when we finally reached our villa, the others had all finished their dinners. We silently appreciated the positive energy projected to us and continued with the rest of the evening as usual.

"Shirin, are you day dreaming, again?" my mother said.

I snapped back to the present and found myself in my room with my diary in my hand, my mother standing over me. "I was just remembering the last time we came to Ramsar."

"I know that this would have been a great opportunity to do that if your father was here, but I think this time we'll settle for having a guest joining us."

Goodness. I had totally forgotten about Ashkan.

"He is coming on Wednesday afternoon, right after school," Mum said before she left my room.

7

I had been so excited all week, not only about having a longer weekend, but also because Ashkan was joining us on Wednesday. I had planned the whole two-and-a-half days in my head over and over again. It had to be right—we could not lose a moment. We had to have enough time to play games, watch videos, go to the park, and listen to Maman bozorg's stories—one each night, which meant two stories. If we were lucky, we would get to hear two stories per night. The snacks had also been carefully planned for and after each activity. We had chips (crisps), *Pofak* (cheese balls), *Yam Yam* (Wafers Choklad), and imported chocolate from abroad.

I even had a look at the menu for the weekend and had offered my input. Maman bozorg had some special dishes that only she could make, and I loved every one of them, but choosing only two dishes out of so many seemed almost impossible. In the end, it was decided: *dolmeh* for one evening, *khoreste zereshk* for another, and pizza for the third evening while watching videos.

I had even brought home a menu of pizzas so we could make our choices before ordering the pizza from next door. Maman bozorg didn't like pizza and did not consider it food. My mum didn't like us eating in front of the television, as we would be breaking one my dad's fundamental rules, but our excitement had spread and they finally gave in.

The videos had to be chosen carefully. Because it was forbidden to watch foreign films, we had to have them smuggled to the house by a young motorcyclist who was mobile and did not have a shop as such. We made a list of videos that were new and chose one for the first evening. For the other, we chose one of our favourites from our own collection at home, one that we had watched a thousand times but could watch a thousand more.

It wasn't an easy task as I had to consider the ages of the viewers and their interests, and it had to be a comedy that we could all enjoy. Therefore, I chose *Chitty Chitty Bang Bang* as the second movie for the weekend.

As for games, we had planned video games with Shahin, as he had been really looking forward to Ashkan's stay. Games such as *Iropoly* (Monopoly) and chess were on the list too.

All day Wednesday I had been listening to my friends telling me about their wonderful and amazing plans for the weekend, and I had been looking forward to our own and feeling proud that I had planned to the last detail.

Feeling quite satisfied, I looked around to see if I had forgotten anything. Then I made my way to the kitchen window and looked for the green Paykan. I could hear the tea simmering quietly, and the saffron rice's scent was making me dizzy from hunger. I knew that my dayee would probably drop Ashkan off and head back, but my mum hoped that he would join us for dinner.

I heard the buzz before I could see the car. I looked down and there they were. My dayee, Ashkan—and who was she?

My mum answered and let them in. I had seen a six-year-old girl stepping out of the car, but didn't know who she was. She was younger than Shahin, but who could she be? *Who cares? I* thought. *Ashkan is here!*

As soon as they entered, the girl disappeared into the hallway that led to the bedrooms while the rest of us were busy greeting each other. Shahin and I were telling Ashkan about our detailed plans for the weekend. The more we said, the more excited all three of us felt, and none of us could believe that the day had finally come. As we were sharing and dreaming ahead, we heard a thump and ran towards the bedrooms, and found the girl in my room on the floor with my doll collection all over her.

"Who is she?" I asked, my voice filled with anger. I didn't wait for an answer but started to pick up my dolls, which I hadn't played with for a long time but had neatly collected them over the years. She took hold of one of them and screamed that that's the one she wants. I didn't give in and said that they were not to be played with. "They are collector's items," I said calmly, trying to be an adult.

She screamed and cried until my mum convinced me to let her have it. "It will only be for a while. The spoilt brat will leave soon," she said. I gave it to her unwillingly, in the hope that she would vanish soon—which she did, along with my dayee and Ashkan.

I didn't understand then what exactly happened, but today I do. Apparently my dayee had asked my mum to look after her *and* Ashkan during weekend, but Mum had refused. She had said that we wouldn't be able to take responsibility for her, and then Dayee had said that he would only leave Ashkan on the condition that she stayed. My mum shook her head, and with that the girl, Ashkan, and my dayee were out of the door. I looked at the back of the car from the window and could see Ashkan waving with his face turned, as if he didn't want us to see his sadness. But I couldn't stop my tears. I sobbed along with Shahin and demanded answers: "Who was she? Why did she have to stay? What happened?"

I soon realised who she was—a thief who had entered our home, taken my cousin, my uncle, and my doll away. I still remember and feel the pain and emptiness of having to face the weekend with this major disappointment.

We sat in the living room in shock, hoping that Dayee would change his mind and come back, perhaps having just have parked around the corner to prove a point. But it was confirmed when he called to say that they had safely arrived home and that we should enjoy our weekend.

We sat in anger and watched the time pass by until Shahin asked for food. We ate in silence until Maman bozorg said, "This will be a good lesson for all of you to learn—especially you, Shirin. We plan and do our best, but sometimes some things are not meant to be. Something beyond our control takes over and we have to make new plans."

Of course she was right. I was so busy planning and so looking forward to the weekend, dreaming about it, that I had not seen this coming. But I was so angry with my dayee that I had to take it out on someone. "Beyond our control? He is your son. Don't you have any control over him? Doesn't he respect your wishes?"

"Shirin, I know you are angry, but this is not the end of the world. We will make news plans."

It was impossible to comfort me. I wanted to crawl under the sheet and weep, but soon she joined me and whispered in my ear: "I am still here! Let's be grateful and make the most of it."

She was right. After all, it was a countdown for her stay too. I hugged her and listened carefully.

"*Yeki bood, yeki nabood*," she began.

> Once upon a time there was a prince who had everything that anyone in his land could ever wish for—wealth, health, youth, and charm—and he was loved by his parents and his people. But he felt that something was missing. He was not happy and didn't seem to appreciate his possessions and gifts in life.
> One day His Majesty, the King, asked to speak to the prince in private. 'Your mother and I have noticed your lack of joy and pleasure in life.'
> The prince looked down and the king continued: 'We have been thinking and we would like to share our thoughts with you.'
> The prince looked up and listened attentively. 'I was going through the same stage as you when I was your age, and my father introduced me to your mother and her family. My life changed and I became so involved with my responsibilities

that I forgot about my sadness. Today I can say with confidence and relief that I was missing a queen and an heir in my life. That's what was missing.'

The prince looked down again. He wanted to say so much; that perhaps that is not what he was missing! What if marriage and fatherhood would not make him happy? He felt that he couldn't speak against his father and had to respect his wishes.

'With your permission, Son, I have the perfect future queen in mind, and I will arrange an invitation for her so you can meet.'

It was now or never. The prince had to speak up. Finally, he gathered his courage and said, 'I have been blessed with such considerate parents to be concerned about my feelings and so thoughtful about my future. Yes, I have been quite unhappy lately. I would like to accept your offer, but I would like to have a little bit more time to explore life outside the palace.'

He sighed and continued: 'I have been thinking that I know so little about the city, the land, and the world. How can I be a good king for my people if I know so little about them? How they live, their wishes, interests, and wants.'

The king nodded and said, 'Son, you have made a very proud father today! You have brought happy tears to my eyes. I wish I had you wisdom.'

'Allow me one month and I will be back to meet the chosen future queen.'

'One month?' the king asked.

'What is thirty days in one's life?'

'I guess I could persuade your mother and convince her of the idea.'

The prince knew that convincing the queen would not be an easy task, but he left it to his father and went to pack for his departure in the morning. He packed his necessities—his shaver, soap, towel, and clean underwear, some food, and enough clean clothes to manage a change. He chose his horse and asked to have him ready by the morning.

Early the next morning, before sunrise, he asked the guards to open the gates, and for the first time he set his feet outside the castle. He was excited and breathed in the air outside the castle. He looked at the sky and appreciated the beauty of the stars as they disappeared in the light of the rising sun.

The prince felt free for the first time—he felt that he had been imprisoned for many years. He thought of his father, who had missed his opportunity to experience some time away from his castle without being recognised as the king. For the fist time, the prince felt happy!

He rode into the light and rode until he reached the next town. He asked for the nearest *mosafer khaneh* (inn) and asked for a room. The room was very simple with a bed and a wash basin. The prince laughed out loud because of the simplicity and how free he felt to live like others.

His next step was to find a job. He asked if anyone knew of a job available in town, and was directed to a shop where they sold fabrics and best wool in the land. He spoke to the owner, and even though he had no experience his charm paid off. He got the job and would start the next day.

The prince knew that he had only a month so he counted the days, but he wanted to stay a while to be able to get to know the town and its people. He decided to stay for a week. Every morning he started his day before sunrise and worked hard until sunset, had his dinner, and went straight to bed. The only privilege he allowed himself was to bathe each evening and relax in the bath. His body would ache from the hard work, his feet would suffer from blisters and cuts from walking and standing all day, and his hands and fingers would bleed from the torture he put them through during the day. But his soul was happy, and he was smiling from within.

He had become so reliable in the eyes of the owner that he was given a set of keys to the shop. Rumour had it that the owner had never done that before. The prince grew in confidence and felt that he missed his life at the palace less and less with each passing day.

One day, the owner called for him and asked for a private moment. He told the prince that tomorrow would be the full moon, and each month on that day a werewolf would attack the town—stores, houses, and people—if he was not fed and given money and wealth.

The prince was shocked to hear this, and by what the shop owner said next: 'I would like to go through this with you, what everyone is going to leave out for him this month.' What shocked the prince the most was that the owner and everyone else seemed so willing to go along with this—were ready to be stripped of their money, food and belongings just to feed a thief's greed.

'Tell me more about the werewolf,' the prince said.

'There isn't much to tell. No one knows what it is or where it comes from. We learned from our fathers and they from their fathers to feed him, as he has attacked the city for many years.'

'So no one has actually seen him? No one knows whether he actually exists or not? Whether it is only a tale made up, to earn an easy living?' asked the prince with sarcasm in his voice.

'I can see that you do not believe in werewolves.'

'I believe in evidence and facts, not hearsay,' replied the prince.

'Even if you would convince me otherwise, there is a whole town full of people who believe their fathers and grandfathers, and it will not be easy to convince them otherwise.'

The prince decided to take action, and by evening he walked back to the store and selected a spot on top of his favourite tree and waited for the arrival of his enemy. By the time the moon showed her beautiful fullness, he heard the loud, unusual howls. As the howls became tighter and closer, the prince's curiosity about the creature grew. He looked around for a first glimpse of the creature, with the bright moonlight as support.

Finally he saw something small moving about—the source of the horrible noise and howling. The prince thought the creature was no bigger than he was, perhaps a little smaller. That made him even more determined to attack it.

The prince had his sword ready in his left hand and decided that it was time to face the enemy who had stolen from the town and the innocent, hard working people. He fell on the creature and grabbed it by its neck, ready to split its upper body, when he heard: 'Wait!'

A man revealed himself to the prince. He took off a mask and revealed that he was only a man in wolf's clothing. The prince dragged him into the centre of town and when the people saw through their windows that it was just a man they felt safe enough to come out of their homes. They gathered around in anger and were shouting and screaming at him for stealing from them. They also expressed their anger at their forefathers and fathers—and at themselves for believing in the tale.

'Who are you?' someone finally asked.

'I am just a humble visitor passing your town and I heard of the myth. Being a poor man, I seized the opportunity to collect money that was so readily given away because of a myth.'

'Wait a minute—how long have you been doing this?' the prince asked.

'Only for a couple of months. I scared off the one before me. He was also a visitor.'

'Let's hang him,' someone yelled. 'No—let's stone him to death,' another shouted.

'Hold on!' the prince interrupted. 'You may be angry with him for stealing, but you did this to yourselves. You stole from yourselves. You gave power to an old tale and made it live for as long as you can remember.'

They let go of the thief and thanked the prince for his wise words and for breaking the superstitious cycle. The prince felt that he had fulfilled his mission, and by the end of that week he was ready to ride to the next town.

He arrived in another small town with people who seemed very happy, generous, and extremely petite in size. The prince was immediately offered a place to sleep and was invited for dinner. He felt that he had a lot to learn from the people and decided to stay.

He was offered a bath and his clothes were washed for him. For dinner he was invited to the centre of the city, where he was the guest of honour.

There was music and dancing before dinner was served, and he could see the lamb being roasted on the grill. The freshly baked bread in the stone oven would be served with yoghurt and aubergine dip. The scent of the saffron rice made the wait unbearable.

The prince soon found out that the feast was in his honour. The generous people of this city would welcome each visitor by inviting them to a feast the very first evening of their arrival, but when the prince found out that visitors usually stayed just a short time, he wondered how they could decline such hospitality and generosity after just a few days.

Just before the meal was served, the prince wondered how the people of this city could be so slim if they threw feasts like this almost every other day in honour of new visitors. It was an amazing mystery!

Feeling tired and hungry from his journey, he was looking forward to the dinner when it was finally served. It was customary for the guest of honour to be served, and he gracefully thanked the hosts for the food and tried a spoon full of rice and lamb. How pleasurable it was as the tastes of cumin, coriander seeds, and saffron played joyfully with his taste buds. He dipped the freshly baked bread into the aubergine dip, and once again closed his eyes to allow his senses to savour the tastes. The prince felt that he must make this town known for having the finest cuisine in the land when he returned to his throne. He washed it down with a sip of red cherry wine.

Feeling as if he were in seventh heaven, he was eager to experience these marvellous taste sensations again. But as he went to have a second spoonful, he noticed that he had reached the bottom of his bowl. He was shocked. He turned his bowl around and upside-down, and it seemed like an ordinary bowl, like many he'd seen on his journey. He looked around and noticed that everyone seemed satisfied with the amount of food they had been given. They had all finished their meal with one spoonful.

Soon all the beautiful and tasty leftovers were packed in bags and left outside the city for the animals. The prince felt a tear in his eyes. All that gorgeous food was wasted, and he was going to bed hungry.

He felt angry and disappointed, as if he had only sniffed the food and was only allowed a taste of what he could not have. He decided not to point out any of this to the people until he had a chance to do a little investigating. None of it made any sense to him, but he was sure that in the daylight he would be able to find out more.

Early next morning, he rose with the pain of hunger in his stomach. He went downstairs for breakfast, and as the scenario was repeated he recalled the night before and realised that it had not been just a bad dream.

The prince had a spoonful of porridge with melted butter and cinnamon on top, washed it down with a small glass of freshly brewed tea, and headed out. He looked for a pottery shop and noticed that there were none in the town. All the pottery and cutlery had been imported to the city many years ago. What intrigued him the most was that people seemed satisfied with the amount of food they were offered and the amount of food wasted each time.

The more the prince looked into this mystery, the less he understood it. He also noticed that people looked paler, lacked energy and didn't seem efficient. He put it down to poor diet.

The prince observed the day and noticed that people would work fewer hours in the day and sleep more as they lacked energy. They'd have a spoonful of breakfast, a spoonful of lunch and the same for dinner. The town was suffering and falling behind its seasonal chores and responsibilities, and that the people complained of a lot of illnesses and pain.

The following day, the prince felt less energetic and fell into a routine of waking up late and not looking forward to his meal. He only sniffed at the food, which was torture enough for him.

He headed to the city centre again and decided to try one of the few restaurants there. He ordered lunch and waited while all the aromas in the kitchen filled the restaurant and made him dizzy from hunger. When the food was served, he examined the bowl and decided it seemed like any ordinary bowl. Next he examined the spoon, and it seemed like any spoon he had ever used. He filled the spoon once, and the bowl was empty.

Suddenly, looking closer at the bowl, he noticed that there was a layer inside of it that he had not noticed before. This made the bowl a lot shallower than it appeared, leaving room for just one spoonful.

He decided to thank the hosts for the food by offering to do the washing up, as they would not allow him to pay. The owner refused, but soon gave in to the prince's determination. Together they collected all the day's bowls, plates, pots, and cutlery, and took them to the nearest river. The prince watched as the owner and the dish-washer boy rinsed them all in the pure water. They took one plate after another and dipped them into the water, then left them to dry. The prince shouted with joy as he figured out the problem: 'You don't wash your dishes properly! That is where the problem lies.'

'What do you mean?' the owner and boy asked the prince in confusion.

'How long have you been washing your dishes that way?'

'I was taught to wash dishes by my father, who was taught by his father, and so on.'

'Of course!' said the prince. He took a bowl and a handful of grass from nearby and started to scrub inside the bowl as hard as he could. Gradually he could see a crack, he and showed it to the others.

'You have broken my bowl,' said the owner.

The prince continued to scrub until the dirt and mould inside the bowl came off bit by bit and the bowl started to look healthier, whiter, and newer. 'You need to have enough nutrition for the amount of work that it is expected of you during your hard working days. It is a shame that all that good food goes to waste—and having the best cuisine that I have ever tasted makes it even more shameful. Your wild animals and pets look healthier than you. Besides, all the pain and illnesses that you are suffering from may originate from the dirt and mould that you eat with your spoonfuls of meals.'

The owner and the boy started to scrub the dishes like never before, and when the dirt and mould fell off they felt joyful and laughed at the simplicity of the solution to a problem they had never before noticed.

They shared the discovery with the rest of the town and threw a farewell feast for the prince on his last night there to thank him. They all enjoyed their meal, and had more than enough of the best meal they'd ever eaten.

The following day, once again fully satisfied at having helped out, he headed to the next town.

When the prince arrived in the next town, he noticed how quiet it was. He was tired and hungry, but his primary concern was for his horse. They had ridden for two days and both were exhausted. As soon as he found a *mosafer khaneh*, he knocked on the door, but it was awhile before he was let in. The owner examined him back and front and asked forgiveness for doing so as soon as they walked through the room.

The prince was already curious about this odd behaviour, but decided to leave it until the morning. After feeling safe about his horse's well-being, he decided to bathe, eat, and crawl under the sheets for a good night's sleep.

The following day, the prince asked for some breakfast and asked the landlady if she knew of a job available in town. The landlady looked at her husband and they both shook their heads.

'How extraordinary,' said the prince. 'A town that has all the jobs taken by its inhabitants. Does this mean that everyone has a job and enough income to provide for their families?' He understood immediately that his curiosity might have given away his real identity, but it was too late to reframe the question, so he waited patiently for an answer.

It seemed that the couple were not interested in satisfying the prince's curiosity, and the prince found this also interesting. He decided to take a tour of the town and make his own discoveries.

As he walked to the town centre, he noticed people were locked indoors, whether at work or at home. Windows were locked, and as soon as someone walked through a door they locked it behind them. People would look around suspiciously when they heard a knock, and if the faces were familiar they would let them, in but if not the stranger would be thoroughly examined.

The prince found it all very intriguing and wanted to have encounter with someone to hear more about their experiences. He found a *ghahve khane* (coffee shop), but soon realised that like every other shop and restaurant in the town, people had to knock, be examined in order to be let in, and be locked in until they were ready to leave.

There was a nice breeze outside and it made the prince sad to think how many times he had taken for granted the pleasure of enjoying his tea, sweet, juicy dates and *gheyloon* (shisha pipe), on Persian Rugs on the veranda. Now he was being locked in a coffee shop in a room full of smoke, where people would quickly finish their teas, smokes, and suspiciously look out the window before leaving.

He found a spot, sat down, caught someone's attention, and tried his best to find out what he could about the strange behaviour of the people here, which didn't seem to bother anyone.

'All I can tell you is to be careful and beware of the man carrying an old man on his back,' said one man he spoke to.

'There is a man who is carrying another man on his back? What for?' asked the prince.

'This town was a happy place once, where people celebrated their annual gatherings and children played until late in their backyards and adults were free to come and go as they pleased. There was laughter and peace, until twenty years ago.

A visitor was passing through the city. The people had such friendly and generous attitudes towards their guests and liked to hear about the world outside the city, so they invited him into their homes, offered him food, a place to stay, and even money for his necessities. He took advantage of their hospitality, and soon people found it tiresome to give but receive nothing back.

After a year, when he felt that he had misused everyone's kind-hearted friendliness, he gathered everyone around in the town centre, thanked them for their patience with him, and asked for forgiveness. He explained that he felt so ashamed for his behaviour that he wanted to leave the town. People felt guilty for not being able to offer him any more, and felt bad for becoming fed up with his requests, so they asked if there was anything else that they could do for him.

He explained that he had not walked for awhile and his feet and legs were stiff, and that he could not go very far. He requested either a horse or someone to carry him out of town.

People discussed this for awhile and decided that it would be best if someone carried him, as a horse would cost the town a fortune. A young and healthy man, Saman, was chosen for this mission, and we all cheered as the man jumped on Saman's back.

The same evening, we were waiting to celebrate Saman's return, and when he did we noticed that he was still carrying the man on his back. Ever since, the man has refused to get off his back. Saman has had to provide for himself as well as the man on his back for almost twenty years.'

The prince was shocked to hear this, and fuming with anger at the same time. 'For twenty years this young's man life and living has been controlled by a thief who refuses to leave him alone,' he thought. 'What a life!'

Then aloud he said, 'There may be many things that I have no understanding of, but tell me why these generous, friendly, kind-hearted people cannot help to get him off Saman's back.'

'We tried once, and it seemed that he wanted to jump off Saman's back right onto someone else's. We needed to protect ourselves and our families. Saman had no family—he is single.'

'And thanks to this thief, he still is. You are all as guilty, in my eyes. Saman is imprisoned by this man while you protect yourselves and shut your eyes to what is happening to him.'

People in the tea room looked at each other, felt embarrassed, and finally asked, 'What are we to do?'

'For one thing, don't lock your selves in and isolate yourselves and Saman. Don't allow the thief to feel more powerful and in control of his game plan,' the prince said.

On the way back to the inn, he was thinking of Saman's life—a young man's life ruined by someone else's greed for easy living. His anger made him determined to end the nonsense and free Saman from this evil as soon as possible.

He left the inn in the early evening, fully prepared to face the evil. He had located Saman's cottage and felt quite relieved to see that he was on his way back from the well.

It was exactly as he had been told and as painful to see as he had imagined. Saman was carrying an old man on his back, and in his hands he had two buckets of water. The old man was complaining of fatigue and that he had not been given enough water and food for the day. Saman was silent and tried his best to reach the door as quickly as possible.

The prince grabbed the man from behind and held him by the neck. 'Step down, or I'll break your neck,' the prince said.

'Please let go of an old man. I am in suffering and this young man is kind enough to help me.'

'Step down or I'll kill you.'

'Do you want me to jump on your back instead? That is what I will do if I step down.'

The prince held his neck even tighter between his hands and twisted it further until he heard a scream. 'Stop!' screamed the old man. 'I will step down.'

As the prince had figured, it would have been very difficult for the old man to get off Saman's back after getting rides for twenty years, much less jump on someone else's. People had fallen for his threats for so many years while he had gotten away with his evil blackmail.

The prince loosened the old man's arms from Saman's chest, his legs from around his waist, and his head from Saman's shoulder. All at once the old man fell down on his bottom. People gathered around and looked at the man who had taken advantage of their friend for so long.

He looked tiny, twisted, and crippled. He had not moved for twenty years. He had been fed, washed, and cared for. Saman's back was bent from the weight that he been carrying.

'Let's kick and beat him to death,' someone said.

'It would not be fair, as he can not defend himself,' said the prince.

'Was it fair when he attacked our city with his evil mind and took a young man's life and imprisoned the rest of us?' they jointly asked.

'I am not defending him, but will it not be enough revenge to leave him as he is? He will not be able to care for himself after twenty years of not doing so. He made himself a cripple.'

Saman was rewarded as the town hero, and a big celebration was held in his name. The prince left the following morning and continued his journey to the next town. He knew that his days away from the castle were numbered and he had to return soon to keep to his promise.

He felt sad to leave the outside world and return to the life chosen for him. During his journey, he had shown wisdom and courage in choosing his direction and making his choices, and he felt he owed it all to the temporary freedom he had been given—the freedom to think freely and to make his own decisions. The thought that he had only a week of that left saddened him.

As he approached the next town, he noticed that he had to enter a gate. He could already hear cheers and celebrations going on in the city. He became fascinated by this and asked the guards to tell him more.

'The *kadkhoda* (mayor) of the town has been blessed with the most beautiful daughter on the face of the earth,' a guard explained. 'She had suitors by the age of fourteen. The suitors would kill for her. This concerned the *kadkhoda*, so he came up with a plan—he would arrange three days of competition for the bachelors of the land who would vie for the love of Pari.

The prince was intrigued and wanted to see the beauty that attracted so many from all over to compete for her. He asked to be let in. Soon he saw the crowd that had gathered and was waiting impatiently to hear about the first task. He finally located Pari, who was sitting on a chair high up so that she would be noticed, and so she could see the men fighting to win her love.

She had beautiful long, curly dark brown hair, beautiful almond-shaped hazel eyes, with plum red cheeks and cherry lips. The prince felt his heartbeat increase. He felt it speaking to him, and knew what it was saying: 'I have fallen in love!'

The prince joined the line for the first competition and learned that they had to transfer a feather from one side of the wall to the other. The other men, full of rage and impatience, used force and power to throw the feather over. Some even used swords, knives, and their muscles to battle with the light feather, until they exhausted themselves and gave up.

The prince calmly waited his turn and gently picked up the light feather and blew on it so that it was given life and started to dance in the air. He blew some more to direct the feather over the wall, and the wind took care of the rest.

The *kadkhoda* was very curious about this young man's wisdom, as he was the only one who had ever passed his first challenge. He decided to invite the prince for dinner so that he could find out more about him.

Pari was also interested to learn more about the man who had completed a challenge created by her father. 'This might be my way out,' she was thinking, but decided to contain her excitement until the evening.

Every year her father planned a three-day event in the city, and every year young eligible bachelors came from near and far to attend and to prove their suitability for marriage. Each time there was a big gathering for the challenges during the day and big dinner parties in the evening.

In all these years no man had completed even the first task created by her father. Each year Pari would wish to be free of these annual gatherings and hope to start her own family, but so far her father had found no one suitable for her.

The *kadkhoda* wanted no more for his daughter than to be happy, and he believed that no money in the world would bring them happiness. That is why he believed that the tasks would prove someone's ability to endure long years of marriage and its hurdles. This year, everyone was fascinated by the young man who had completed the first day's task, which was unheard of.

Music and entertainment were a big part of the evening event. Good food and wine were served, along with deserts and sweets. The prince's eyes caught Pari's for a moment, and knew for sure that he had fallen in love with her. He also knew that he was going to do all in his power to marry her. He worried about the next task, but based on today's task, he felt confident that he understood what the *kadkhoda* was looking for.

He woke up early next morning and walked up to the hill that overlooked the city. He felt privileged to be experiencing the land and its beauty, with its beautiful sea, rivers, mountains, nature, and the cultures that varied from town to town.

With lungs filled with fresh air, he made his way down to the centre of the town. He listened to the task being announced and noticed how the other competitors reacted as they lined up—overconfident that they could prove themselves suitable for Pari.

The competitors were presented a question: 'Which is heavier—one kilo of wool, or one kilo of lead?' One by one young bachelors stepped up and offered their answer, and one by one they were rejected.

The prince, who had joined the end of the line, offered his answer: 'Neither. They both weigh the same—one kilo.' A cheer of joy rose up from the crowd—he had made it to the next and final round.

Pari was hoping to have a moment to speak to her possible future husband, but at the same time she didn't want to get her hopes up, in case he failed the final task. She was aware that it was the most difficult of all. But the prince caught Pari's eyes once again, and they knew that their love would overcome that final obstacle tomorrow.

First thing in the morning, the prince prepared himself mentally for the next task and listened carefully as it was announced. The reactions were different. Some felt that they had to give up as they saw no point in continuing, some felt overconfident, and others just wanted to try their luck.

They were all escorted to the seaside, and the *kadkhoda* pointed out the spot where his beloved dead wife's wedding ring had gotten lost. Their task was to find it. 'Impossible,' said some. 'That happened ten years ago. How can anyone find it today?' Others said, 'It might have even been washed to the neighbouring country.'

Some didn't waste any time and got busy looking for the ring, jumping into the sea and swimming as far as they could. Those who wanted to try their luck near the shore started their search carefully and with patience. The prince chose a spot, sat down, and observed all that was going on.

By late afternoon, some had given up and some had left, while others were still trying their luck. What they had not noticed though was that the tide had gone out. The prince stood up and walked around the beach where the sea had been earlier. He looked around and continued until he reached the rocks at the end of the beach. He looked back and noticed how far he had come. He closed his eyes, took in the fresh sea breeze, and imagined walking with Pari to the seaside, the two of them promising to love and hold each other throughout all eternity.

He asked his heart to direct him to the ring. 'If our love is strong enough, the power of our love will lead me to the ring,' he thought.

Finally, just as the sun was about to set, he felt satisfied that he could trust his instincts. He opened his eyes and followed the directions his heart had given, and he saw something shiny—something that was still metres away bright enough to guide him.

At last he picked up the ring and knew that his love for Pari had led him to it. Their love was united, and no one could come between them now.

They celebrated their wedding ceremony for forty days and forty nights, with the *kadkhoda* and the king and queen at their sides. People from all over the land joined the celebrations and offered their best wishes.

The prince and Pari promised to serve their people and preserve their freedom forever.

"I love you, Maman bozorg."

"So do I, Dear—so do I. Good night."

"*Shab bekheyr!*"—Good night.

8

Though we were disappointed, the following day we decided to stick to our plans and go to the park. We missed Ashkan, but Maman bozorg said that we had to come to terms with our fate for this weekend. Still, we sighed and expressed our unhappiness.

"There must be a reason for the change of plans this weekend," she consoled us.

"I know that it makes you feel better when you say that, but I don't find it even slightly comforting," I argued.

"In my experience, there is always a good reason for a sudden change in the original plans. At the time we may feel very disappointed, but I have learned to believe that when it is not meant to be, it is just not meant to be—and all for a good reason. We just have to trust and accept it. A child who wants to run and chase a friend in the middle of the street will certainly be stopped by his parents or guardians." Maman bozorg looked at me, waiting for my reply.

I just nodded.

"You also must agree with me that the children will become very disappointed and angry for being stopped. The adults are responsible for their safety and must do what is best for the children, no matter how disappointed and angry they may feel."

"I don't understand the reason for the change in our plans for this weekend," I said, shaking my head.

"I know, and that hurts. You have to trust that there must have been a good reason."

I made the most of the day with Shahin, and when we finally had enough of chasing each other, swinging, and walking through the beautiful Melat Park, with its heavenly scenery—the man-made lake and the gorgeous white and black swans swimming in it, the rose garden and the flower shows—we each treated ourselves to *balal* (barbecued corn on the cob) dipped in salt water and found pleasure in every little kernel.

§§§§§

On the way home, my mum asked if we should invite Meme for dinner, and we all agreed that it was a wonderful idea.

We ordered pizza on the way home, and when we arrived we sat around the dining table and sampled different slices from all the boxes. Shahin and I enjoyed every slice, some more than others. Meme and Maman bozorg struggled with the texture and taste, and finally they had good laugh about it.

Mum asked, "Shall we save some for Baba?" (She called my father's father "Baba.")

My grandmothers burst into laughter, like a couple of school children. They treated it as a joke shared between the two of them, as if we wouldn't understand, yet Shahin and I joined in.

"Where is he, anyway?" my mum asked, trying to interrupt the ridiculous laughter, obviously tired of it.

"He is out with his friends," Meme said, wiping off her tears of laughter. "I needed the laugh," she continued. "I was lonely and bored at home. You must have sensed that I was desperate for company and laughter.

"Men!" said my Maman bozorg. "They come and go as they please. Can we do that? Can we say, 'Honey, I am going out with my friends, see you when I get back. And don't wait up.'?"

The picture she painted must have pushed yet another laugh button, because now all the women in the room burst into laughter. But the feminist power in the room became apparent when the laughter eventually faded and the women began planning to teach the men a lesson. It was fascinating to listen to their plans of a strike, such as locking them out, not answering their phone calls, or even ignoring their needs.

They spent the rest of the evening detailing their plans and making a pact. The newly empowered women celebrated their premature victory over a cup of tea with freshly baked Danish pastries.

When the phone rang, they pretended they didn't hear and talked over the ringing. Soon it went over to the answering machine, and we could hear my dad's worried voice: "Shahla Jaan? Where are you all? You should be home by now…All right, I will call again.

Mum couldn't resist and picked up the phone the second time it rang, and told my dad that we had been in the garden and that we were all fine.

Maman bozorg couldn't resist my dayee's third attempt to call and picked up the phone to put him out of his misery. Meanwhile, Meme couldn't resist my grandfather's constant knocking and banging on the door and finally gave in.

The women looked at each other and shrugged their shoulders. "Well! At least we tried," said one. "We cannot change the world in one day," said another. "At least we have shown them that we have some say in it too," said the third.

I felt the least I could do would be to go to bed and let them be happy and deluded in their fantasy world, where they had gained power over their men.

9

Amoo picked me up after school and after lunch I locked myself in my room, as I usually did before an exam. I would not let myself out unless I had to use the bathroom. I would have a meal pack prepared for me in case I got hungry or thirsty—then I could eat in my room without being disturbed. No rest during study time was allowed. Even though I had learned from experience that you can only do so much the day and night before exams, somehow I felt better prepared if I went through all that pain and torture.

Of course my mind wandered off now and then, and had daydreams about my plans for the future, but I usually picked up from where I had left off and continued.

Long after dark, when the clock showed eleven, I was making my way to the bathroom to brush my teeth and to get ready for bed when I heard a melancholy song in the darkness. I recognised my mother's voice as she sang a song I'd heard many times before—like when my father's uncle passed away, or the night before my Baba Bozourg's (Mother's father) memorial service each year, or when Shahin was ill in the hospital.

"Mum, why are you singing in the dark?" I asked as I walked towards the sound of her voice. The moonlight through the window dispelled the darkness somewhat, and I could see her sitting by the window, looking out.

I felt that I had missed part of the day by being locked in my room. I had heard the phone ringing a couple of times, but never thought it was bad news.

My hands felt wet when I touched her face and realised that she had been crying. "Maman Jaan"—Dear Mum—"tell me what is wrong!" I said, thinking that I hated that song and wishing she would stop.

She sighed and finally said that there had been an attack in the south of Iran, one of the worst since the start of the war. I thought of my father, and for a moment I went deaf. I couldn't hear my mum and could barely see her lips moving in the dark, but I could hear the freaking song in my head.

I thought about how disobedient I had been during his absence, how I had let him down and disappointed him. I thought of all the rules that I had broken—eating in front of the television, sleeping on the roof top, eating unhealthy food such as pizza. I had bought snacks from vendors on street corners—home-made and home-packed sour cherries and plums. (My dad always warned us about them—"You don't know who made them and where their hands have been," he would say.) I missed a couple of piano lessons, forgot to brush my teeth a few times, fell behind in my studies on days after having indulged in movies and snacks, forgot not to speak while I was eating, forgot to use cutlery in the "correct way," had not been as polite as I should have been on the phone when I answered (I'd been taught phone etiquette), forgot to empty the bin in my room a couple of times, and once I had even walked home all by myself after having waited an hour for my ride.

Finally, my mother's lips stopped moving.

"Mum, is Dad alive?" I asked impatiently, hoping that she wouldn't realise that I had ignored her effort to answer my question.

"We don't know, Darling, we don't know. As I said, the communication lines are cut off. These are difficult times for all of us." She held me in her arms.

Maman bozorg joined us soon with freshly brewed tea and turned the lights on. "Honestly," she said, "I don't understand you two. You are already planning the funeral and burying the poor man alive."

She poured the tea equally in each glass, and I noticed it wasn't just any tea but a special tea—*gole gav zaban*. The tea is known for its calming effects. When it is served, you know that desperate measures are called for, that there is a need for more than just comfort but something less than antidepressants.

"Did you know that Rostam is the great warrior from the Shahnameh?" Maman bozorg said. "Your father's name was chosen especially for him. Your Meme told me that she had him when she was only seventeen years old. Back in those times, medications such as antibiotics were not available in Iran yet and people would die from simple infections. Many infants passed away at birth or later from diseases that went undiagnosed.

"Your grandparents chose his name carefully and named him Rostam—the greatest warrior of all time, according to Ferdowsi as he wrote in his Shahnameh—in the hope that he would survive anything. According to your Meme, he has survived a lot during his life so far. We just have to trust that he will survive it this time too."

"Tell us about the Shahnameh," I pleaded.

"You just don't miss an opportunity, do you."

"It will take our minds off things."

"The Shahnameh was written by Ferdowsi, who was a great believer in Persia and Persians. He wrote the tales of Zaal, Simourgh, Sohrab, Rakhsh, Rostam—and it goes on and on. The Shahnameh has survived many centuries of war and various political beliefs. You can read the easier versions as children's tales, read the Shahnameh as it is—in form of poems—and when it is told by experienced and professional story tellers, it is called: Naghali. People use examples from the Shahnameh and learn lessons from it. It is a pride and joy in our nation."

"Tell us a story from it."

"Shahnameh is too long—it would take more than an evening to tell it all."

"It's okay—you can start tonight and continue another day."

"It is okay now, is it?!"

"Please, Maman bozorg? Please?"

The story goes that Sam Nariman, the great hero of his time, had only one wish—and that was to father a son. He was blessed one day with the news of his wife giving birth to a boy.

Zaal was born with white hair and a body that shone like silver. The handsome baby was kept away from Sam because they all feared his reaction.

Finally the news about the silver-coloured, happy, handsome baby reached Sam, and when he walked into the nursery and had one look at the baby, he rejected him.

'Why have you punished me this way, God?' he yelled out. 'The great hero Sam Nariman will become a laughing stock. This will destroy me!'

He ordered his men to take Zaal far away. His men followed his orders and took him to the Alborz Mountain, and left him on the top of the mountain for the wild animals.

Baby Zaal lay there in the heat of the burning sun, at times crying and at times sucking his fingers for comfort. Simourgh, a beautiful, wise, and powerful bird with a thousand coloured feathers, was leaving her nest to find food when she saw Zaal and picked him up as a meal for her children.

As soon as she put him down to be served, she heard a voice: 'Beware, wise bird—you have in your hands the father of Rostam, the greatest hero of all times. Mother him well!'

Simourgh named him Dastane Zand. The baby birds grew fond of him and called him *Dastan* for short. Zaal grew to become a handsome young man who eventually learned many skills from his mother, the great Simourgh.

Soon news of a handsome, young man with a reputation for many skills had spread throughout the land and reached Sam. He had not forgiven himself for abandoning Zaal and wanted to find his son and ask for forgiveness.

Sam rode to the Alborz Mountain and called for Zaal, asking for forgiveness and begging and pleading for his son to return. Simourgh heard him and understood that he had come for Dastan. She explained to Zaal that Sam was his father and had come for him, and it was time that he returned to his father.

Zaal was disappointed. 'Have you become bored of me, mother? Do you want to be rid of me?' he asked.

'The time has come for us to part, but I will always be with you.' Simourgh gave Zaal one of his feathers and added, 'If you are ever in trouble, burn my feather and I will come and rescue you. You are my child and I will always protect you.'

On that note, Zaal greeted his father and followed him home. Sam Nariman celebrated his son's return and crowned him as the Zaal Zar—the Golden Albino.

"Enough for one evening," Maman bozorg said. "You better go to bed! Do you not have an exam tomorrow?"

"Huh? What happened to the rest of the story?" I complained.

"I told you that it is a long story. Ferdowsi, the great poet, worked on Shahnameh for thirty years."

"But we didn't even reach the tale of Rostam. All I heard was that Zaal was going to father him, which would make Sam his grandfather."

"You told me to start from the beginning, and I will continue another evening."

"Tell me if Simourgh's feather will come to use! And who Rakhsh is. Oh, and if Sohrab was the son of Rostam."

"The Shahnameh is full of tales of great heroes, kings, Deeves, and fairies, each tale more fascinating than the other. To answer your questions: Rostam became a warrior at a young age. Rakhsh was a horse—he had been carefully chosen for the great hero and was very protective of Rostam.

"Simourgh's feather will come to use in extreme and desperate need. Sohrab was Rostam's son, but that is a long and fascinating story itself."

As I was trying to figure out how to convince her to tell me a bit more, the phone rang. On the second ring, we all jumped and ran in different directions towards phones. Then I heard my mum shouting in joy.

My father had managed to reach the nearest city where the communication lines were intact, and he was to let us know that even though a lot of innocent people had died during the attack, he was lucky to escape.

10

Once again I was to learn that studying hard the night before didn't lead to a good grade, but depended more on my effort and concentration in class.

On the way home, my amoo asked me about last night and our worries about losing my father. I didn't feel like talking about it though, as it would be another reminder of my feelings, but I didn't want to be rude and not say anything so I used a polite Iranian approach and said, "Thank God he is safe and well!"

"You can say that again. We were all worried sick about him. So many people died during that attack, you know."

I tuned out and just nodded occasionally to seem interested. Instead I focused on the school children who were walking home for lunch, and wondered what we had for lunch today. It usually took me a while to wake up in the mornings as I was not a morning person, and I could rarely eat in the mornings. I was told that breakfast was the most important meal of the day, but I could never understand that as I didn't really enjoy a meal that early in the day—unless it was one of Maman bozorg's wonderful breakfasts. I would sit by the kitchen table, put sugar in my tea, and stir and stir to buy time until I was told off. So by lunchtime I was absolutely starving.

When we turned onto our road I noticed a lot of people gathered at our door. My amoo parked in the street because he couldn't drive into the garage—there were too many people in the way.

I jumped out of the car as soon as the car stopped, made my way through the crowd, and finally saw my mum in the doorway. She pulled me in and, without asking questions, I made my way through to the second floor. I found Shahin in Maman bozorg's arms.

"What is happening?" I asked.

"Sit down and I'll pour you a cup of tea."

"No more tea. What has happened? I want to know."

"Well, you know how worried we were about your father last night?" I nodded. "The people downstairs were worried too, as news spreads very fast, and they all wanted to make sure that you father is safe and well."

I sat down and let out a deep breath of relief. "Who are they?" I asked.

"Some we know and some we don't. But they all have one thing in common. They all, for one reason or another, could not afford their own or their family's various forms of medical treatments, and your father helped. I ran to the kitchen window, and as soon as I looked down I recognised our *Nafti*—the gas man—who, I remembered, had a daughter who needed an eye operation almost immediately to save her eye. I recognised our cleaner's son who, I remembered, needed a caesarean operation for his wife at the very last minute, but didn't have the money for the procedure. Many of them I didn't know and didn't recognise."

I couldn't see my mum in the doorway, but could hear her reassuring them of my father's safety and thanking them greatly for coming and paying their respects.

"When is he coming home?" one of them asked.

"Soon! Next week some time. I will forward your regards this evening, when I speak to him. I am sure that he would like to see you all when he comes home."

"Shirin! It is rude to look out the window like that!" I heard my Maman bozorg say loudly. "I am sure that we will soon hear it all from your mother."

While in the sitting room I heard, a "baa," followed soon by another one and then in choir with a few "*Ghooghoolighoo*" (that is the sound of a cock in Farsi). Confused, I looked at Shahin and Maman bozorg. Shahin started to giggle, and it made me think that he was playing a trick, but that was so unlike Shahin. Shahin and Maman bozorg, seeing my expression and body language, both laughed until their eyes were teary. I decided to leave them to their foolishness and follow the animal noises from the balcony facing our garden, where I could see the animal farm out there.

"Dad will go crazy," I yelled out. I thought back to when I was four years old and received a white rabbit as a gift from Ms.

Flinten, who was my beautiful nursery school teacher. I loved her, and therefore decided to accept the rabbit when it was offered to us—even though its red eyes scared me. As soon as my father came home it was returned. He explained that there was no space for pets inside, and outside it would ruin the garden's beautiful and rare plants.

I looked at our garden, with the lamb on one side and the chickens, hens, and cocks surrounding the Sharon tree, the beautiful yellow rose plant and monkey flowers. I loved our roses, mostly the one on the arch as it was a unique yellow colour. We were not supposed to offer yellow flowers to anyone because it apparently meant "I don't like you." Nevertheless, it gave the garden such rare beauty. The monkey flowers resembled monkey faces, and I loved to put my fingers inside its mouth and pretend that it was biting me. The persimmon tree offered us the most gorgeous Sharon fruit in autumn, and we loved to munch on them when they were ripe.

"What are we going to do?" I heard my mother ask from the balcony.

I just shook my head. "Why did you accept it?"

"These are gifts from people with a lot of gratitude and respect for the help and support that they received from your father. I couldn't reject their gifts and their beautiful gestures."

"The neighbours will complain soon," I said, looking around.

"We need to come up with a solution quickly."

Later that evening the dilemma was discussed with my father and he suggested taking the livestock to the butcher and offering the meat to the needy.

Thanks to all the noises and sounds coming from the garden, it was a long night. The cocks woke me up extremely early, which gave me enough time to develop an appetite by breakfast time, and for the first time I enjoyed breakfast at home before school.

My dayee took care of the animals while we were at school.

§ § § § §

We had only a few days before Dad's return to prepare for celebrations. I found it to be a good distraction, and it brought the family together to focus on something positive—a celebration for his return to safety. Special French pastries were ordered, as were seasonal fruits and fresh vegetables and other ingredients for the meal.

The topic of the day had changed, and all we could think and talk about were the menu, guest list, and the date and time of the event, which kept changing from one evening to the next. It had become a game of distraction that might continue until my father's return.

I was happy to be involved, but I couldn't help feeling somewhat sad. I knew that Dad's return meant that Maman bozorg would leave, if not the same day, then only a few days or at most a week later. Based on past experiences, I imagined our conversation would go something like this: "Your dad is home now and needs to spend time with his family. Things need to get back to normality for all of you, and I need to get back to normality also. You can still come and visit me on Fridays."

And I would say, "But that is not the same as having you here with us. It isn't as if you can tell me your stories or your wise words when I need them the most."

She would then say, "You can always call me. I speak to your mum everyday."

"It is not the same and it is so unfair because you see Ashkan every day and I have to wait until Fridays to see you."

"Your Meme lives on the first floor, and you see her every day." That would be the end of our discussion, and I would curl up in bed and start the grieving process.

Because I knew from past experience the process and discussions that led to the grieving process, I decided to jump right to the part where I would silently struggle with the conflict between my happiness for my dad's return and my sadness over Maman bozorg's departure—the mixed feelings about returning to normality.

As if she had been reading my thoughts, Maman bozorg said, "I will also miss you," and put her arms around me.

I cried and didn't want to let go.

"*Yeki bood, yeki nabood*," she began.

> Once upon a time there was a happy couple living in a cosy house filled with love and happiness, expecting their first child. When the time had arrived, the midwife was summoned and the waiting period began. After seventeen long hours of labour, they could hear a cry and they cheered with joy.
> Because the baby, with her dark blue eyes and beautiful red lips, was the centre of attention, her mother's last gasp for breath went unnoticed.
> When Suri reached the age of five, her father remarried. She was used to being the centre of her father's world and felt complete with the parental love her father offered her. But now she realised that she had to share that with her stepmother—and soon after, with her new half-sister, Farideh.
> Suri found this very difficult, but not as difficult as when she realised that all the household duties and chores were

gradually falling on her shoulders as her stepmother became busy with the new baby, and when her chores no longer allowed her to eat dinners with her family and attend family outings and gatherings.

Seventeen years later, the news about her stepmother expecting their second child was spread. Her father was overjoyed by the news, as it had been seventeen years since they had been blessed with Farideh.

One day Suri was sent to find wild red berries, as her stepmother had urgent cravings for them. Suri made her way to the woods early in the morning with a packed lunch and some water.

She knew the woods well and had become one with its sounds, movements, and smells. She felt safe there, and soon she found the berry bushes. She saw right away that there were very few berries left on them. She continued until she came to a second hidden place where there were berries, and was once again she was disappointed. After lunch she decided to continue a bit farther—unknown territory for her, since she had never gone that deep into the woods.

She could see the bushes from afar, with wild berries hanging on them, shining like red rubies. She soon picked enough to fill her basket. She felt proud of her discovery and courage. It seemed that not even birds and other animals were interested in the berries in this part of the woods.

The berries seemed so juicy and ripe, the biggest that she had ever seen, so she decided to eat a few now that her basket was full. She had reached for the last one, thinking that it would be enough, but decided she wanted more. Searching deep into the bushes, she noticed a castle behind them. She looked around and saw that she was standing in a great garden.

The garden was overgrown, the gate was hidden, and the castle seemed to be deserted. She decided to have a closer look and went all the way through the bushes to the other side. She was amazed at the size of this beautiful castle.

Every time she thought she would leave, though, she found something else that intrigued her, and finally surrendered to her curiosity. She turned the knob on the door, and with some difficulty managed to open it. Standing in the doorway, she called out but, as she had guessed, the castle was deserted. The spider webs, the dust, and dirt spoke of years of neglect.

Suri decided to have a look around. On the first floor she found the kitchen, drawing room, game room, and dining room. When she became bored she made her way upstairs. She started from left to right and visited each room, imagining the inhabitants and wondering who they might have been, why they left, and if they would ever come back to reclaim their property.

She thought of her life and how it had been given over to looking after others—imprisoned in her own home. She thought about living in the castle and making it her home, keeping it clean and safe until its rightful owners returned. She had nothing to lose, and her freedom to gain.

By the third day of her stay, she had managed to clean the rooms, the furniture, and the decorations on the ground floor. By the time she settled in there, she felt she practically needed to start cleaning all over again. But her sense of freedom gave her enough energy to cope with all the work that she had created for herself.

After she had cleaned the rooms on the second floor to her satisfaction, she noticed a narrow hall that she hadn't seen before. There was only one narrow door in the hall, and when her curiosity got the better of her, she tried the doorknob—but it wouldn't turn.

She looked through the keyhole and noticed a body on a bed, and the sight of it made her jump. She took a hair pin from her hair, put it in the keyhole, and jiggled it around. Soon enough, it opened. A handsome young prince was on the bed covered with needles. She tried to rouse him, but he seemed to be unconscious.

Suri noticed a *lohe* that said, 'Read this carefully—Prince Arsalan is a prisoner of the black witch Siahbar. Arsalan has been cursed by ninety needles on his body. No more than one needle can be removed each day, and by the end of the ninetieth day the prince will rise and be alive again.'

Suri removed a needle, cleaned the room, and left it until the following day, when she visited him again and removed another needle.

As the days went by, she began to feel affection for the prince, and looked forward seeing him and removing a needle. There were so many things to do and so little company around the house, so she started to spend more and more time in the room. She started to tell Arsalan her life story, from the day she had been born until the day she had found him.

Every day, when she finished her chores, she would join him to tell a bit of her life story and remove a needle. She would tell him about how she missed having a mother, how ashamed and guilty she felt for being the cause of her death, how she felt about her father blaming her, and how he had pushed her aside when she was five. She talked about how her stepmother and half-sister treated her—the beatings and punishments, locking her in, torturing her with heated spoons and cutlery and leaving burns on her body, then threatening to harm her father if she told him. Suri cried when she told her story, but afterward she felt lighter and would remove a needle.

The days did not pass quickly enough for Suri, and she dreamt of the day that Arsalan would wake up and see her. When Suri looked at herself in mirror, she saw a young, tall, fully developed woman with long dark hair, blue eyes, white skin, and plum red lips.

Suri had become fond of Arsalan and imagined him to be very kind, generous and intelligent, and she could see that he was very handsome.

She had found immense relief through her 'talking cure,' but she knew that if Arsalan had been conscious she would never have dared reveal her innermost thoughts and feelings. She decided to call him 'Sange Saboor'—the patient stone.

As the days brightened, Suri decided to occupy herself in the beautiful garden and attend to it. She spent her days there weeding, trimming the bushes, and seeing to the plants. It made her happy to see the castle finally coming alive and the garden smiling as she looked out through a window. Evenings she would spend with her Sange Saboor and begin where she had left off the previous day, then remove a needle and kiss him goodnight.

When the needles became easy to count, she knew that she had to make the castle immaculate, and therefore decided to spend some time washing the outside walls of the castle so that it would regain its shine. It was hard work, and she knew that she had only a few days left before the last needle was removed.

When there were two only needles left, Suri felt a surge of excitement—but also fear. 'What if he doesn't like me? What if he is not what I imagined him to be? What if he is a horrible and mean prince, and that is why he was cursed by the Siahbar?'

The following day, she put the finishing touches to the house and spent the evening recounting her feelings and thoughts with him, and finally said, 'My Sange Saboor, I will just have to trust you to be as patient and kind as I have made you to be in my mind.' Then she removed one of the two remaining needles and noticed that he moved.

She spent the last day cooking and preparing a celebratory dinner. She planned to take a bath and dress up in a dress she had chosen from the wardrobe upstairs. Then she would do her hair and finally remove the last needle. She wanted to make a good first impression. But towards the afternoon she heard noises from upstairs and decided to look into it before she bathed. As soon as she entered the narrow hallway she heard a female voice that she recognised—and couldn't believe her ears.

'I must be dreaming,' she thought to herself as she opened the door and immediately found herself in a nightmare. But it was all too real. Her half-sister, Farideh was standing in the middle of the room and had removed the last needle, which she still held between her fingers.

'Who are you?' Arsalan asked.

'She is my maid,' Farideh said, not allowing Suri to speak. 'Why are you standing there like plum jam? Greet our prince and bring the tea.'

'What I had to go through, Arsalan Jaan, to see this day, Farideh continued. 'You need to regain your strength, but when you are ready, I will show the castle and the garden. I made sure that it looks exactly like the day you went to sleep. Nothing has changed. You have not missed anything.'

'How can I thank you enough for what you have done for me and for how you have suffered?' Arsalan asked.

'The biggest wedding in the land will have to do as a token of your appreciation.'

Suri was not dreaming—it was all real, and once again she had been robbed of her life, her dignity, and the person she had fallen in love with. All of her efforts had gone to waste as her half-sister had taken credit for it all. How could this be?

On the way to the kitchen, she thought about leaving, but where would she go? Back home to her stepmother? She surely could not stay here and wait upon her stepsister and the love of her life. She was devastated, but she decided to stay for a while—at least until she found enough strength to leave.

She brought dinner to the dining room, followed by dessert. She had not been allowed to bathe, dress nicely, sit at the dining table, or speak. Whenever Arsalan asked Suri a question, Farideh would answer for her.

The following morning, Suri had a visit from Farideh, who gave her a warning: 'One word from you and I will kill Arsalan, and all of this will be mine. If you care for him, you will keep quiet.'

'How did you find me?' Suri asked.

'You silly girl—I wasn't looking for you! No one missed you, not even your cleaning or your help around the house. You were stupid enough to make the beautiful castle visible and shiny so that it attracted my attention. When I read the *lohe*, I knew that all I needed to do was to remove the last needle and all of this would be mine.'

Arsalan had found enough strength to dress himself and look around the castle. He appreciated all the work that had been done to keep it as it was. As soon as he found Suri, he rushed to her and said, 'I wanted to thank you too. You must be responsible for all the actual work, the cleaning, the gardening, and so forth.'

Suri nodded, accepting his gratitude. She remembered Farideh's words.

'This may seem strange,' the prince said, 'but your smell is very familiar to me.'

'You recognise my smell?' Suri asked, forgetting her sister's threats.

'Now I recognise your voice, too.'

'Sange Saboor,' Suri whispered.

> '*You* are the one who looked after me,' the prince said incredulously. '*You* are the one who did all this. She is just a thief stealing it all from us!'
> 'She is my half-sister, and she threatened to kill you if I told you.'
> 'Not if I kill her first,' said Arsalan—and with those words, Farideh was driven out of the castle.

"And they lived happily ever after?" I asked.

"Not really!" said Maman bozorg. "Farideh was feeling so angry at the loss of the wealth that she found Siahbar, the witch, and told her how her half-sister, the evil Suri, had broken the curse. Siahbar, who actually had unfinished business with the King, made her way to the castle and kidnapped the prince on his wedding night."

"Don't tell me that that is the end of the story," I moaned, and Maman bozorg continued.

> Suri woke up to an empty bed and realised that her prince had been taken away from her. With some gold coins, water, and food, she started searching for her husband. She walked through the woods without fear because she had always felt safe there. It was her breathing space and her hiding place when she needed to escape her stepmother's abuse.
> She saw a white cottage shining through the trees and decided to knock on its door. A small, old, bent lady opened the door.
> 'I was wondering where I could find Siahbar,' Suri asked.
> 'How naïve you are!' the old woman said. 'You can't just knock on a door asking for Siahbar!'
> 'Do you know where I can find her?' Suri asked, ignoring her comment.
> 'Come in before you make a bigger fool of yourself.' Once Suri was seated, the old woman said, 'What business do you have with Siahbar?'
> 'She has kidnapped my husband.'

'Are you talking about the prince who was cursed many years ago?'

'I broke the curse, and now she has kidnapped him,' Suri said.

'You may need to accept your destiny,' the old woman said, looking down.

'I have already fought for him once, and I am prepared to do it again. I will not give up.'

'No one has ever won a battle with Siahbar. She was in love with Arsalan's father, the king, but when he married someone else, she promised to make his life a living hell. Siahbar spent her whole life ruining the king's life. The more she tried, the more attached the king and the queen became to each other—until the day she cursed Arsalan. The queen died of heartache and the king became so ill that he called Siahbar to his deathbed and asked for mercy on his son. It was then that Siahbar agreed to allow Arsalan life only if he was found by someone who would patiently remove the needles, one each day without any interruptions.'

'I love Arsalan and I will fight for him,' Suri said with determination.

'Either love or naïveté has blinded you. Either way you are a fool,' said the old woman, shaking her head.

'Can you help me find Siahbar?'

'Someone must have watched over you to guide you to me. Siahbar has many spies, and that is how she has survived for so long, I believe. I will help, but I have little confidence in you,' she said, looking at Suri from head to toe. 'Now listen carefully—I will only say this once. Siahbar is unreachable! Don't focus on finding her. She will find you as soon as she realises that you are on a mission to free Arsalan. Siahbar has left out *lohes* to guide you to him, and as soon as you find him she will be there to stop you.

'You need a couple of things with you, and you will realise when and how to use them when the time comes.' The old woman handed Suri a comb, a mirror, a jar of saltwater, and wrapped pieces of salted dried meat. 'Do not reason with Siahbar when you meet with her—and, last but not least, keep yourself as thin as you are. Try to manage with one meal a day.'

Suri was grateful to the old woman for all the support that she had offered and agreed with her that someone was looking after her so that she didn't get caught up with one of Siahbar's spies and to be led astray.

When she had reached the first *lohe*, it said, 'Welcome to the entrance to hell. This is your last opportunity to turn around. If you still would like to continue your journey, carry straight on to the next *lohe*.'

Farther along another *lohe* read: 'Arsalan is a prisoner of Siahbar, and you will find him in Siahbar's castle right next to the next *lohe*.' Suri felt excited as she got closer to Arsalan, but at the same time her fears were kicking in. 'What if Siahbar cannot be defeated? She must know that I have broken the curse once, and therefore expects me with an even more detailed plan and no room for mistakes to destroy me,' Suri thought to herself.

Suri continued her journey, when she decided that life without Arsalan would not be worth living. She might as well risk her life to save her Sange Saboor.

As soon as she reached the castle gate, she read the *lohe*: 'This is where Prince Arsalan is kept as a prisoner, and there will be no turning back if you enter.'

Resolute, Suri stood there until the gates opened and she was let in. Inside the castle she was welcomed by the vicious Siahbar—an old, evil woman full of hate and anger, who tried her best to appear welcoming to her prisoner. 'My dear child! Do you really want to be a prisoner again? Haven't you had enough imprisonment? Do you really want to waste the rest of your life here?'

Suri remembered the old lady's advice about not reasoning with Siahbar. Instead she just said, 'I have come for my Arsalan.'

'Take it from me! Look what love has done for me! I have been a prisoner of love myself for many years.'

'I have come for Arsalan,' she said again, ignoring Siahbar's words. At this, Siahbar ordered her to be taken upstairs and locked away with the prince.

Suri threw herself on Arsalan, who was lying unconscious on the bed. She cried as she held him in her arms. 'I will save us from here. I will take you far away from Siahbar for good. I promise. Just hold on a while longer,' she whispered in his ears, hoping that he would hear her.

Looking around, she noticed that the room was covered with large windows, and when she looked out one of them, she noticed for the first time that they were imprisoned on the highest point of the castle on top of the biggest hill she had ever been on. Looking down, she saw that the castle was surrounded by water, as if it was an island itself.

Suri sighed, looked at Arsalan, and said, 'At least I am here with you—even if it would mean to be imprisoned for the rest of our lives.'

Just then there was a knock on the door, and Suri jumped up to answer it. She was pleasantly surprised to find a trolley full of food, sweets, and pastries—and all very well presented. She was attracted to a plate full of her favourites, but she remembered the old lady's advice: 'Try to keep as thin as possible.'

Feeling disappointed and angry, but mostly hungry, she understood that the trolley of food was a trap rather than a generous offer from Siahbar. She decided to hide the food away in one of the closets, to make it look like as though she has eaten the meal offered to her.

The more the gestures of hospitality were repeated, the more certain she was that it was a trap, and she played the game well. It gradually became easier to reject the food and just have a bite or two to maintain her energy.

Then one day she woke up to the prettiest sight she had ever seen—a most beautiful large bird outside one of the windows. She smiled and thought that she was dreaming, but when she opened her eyes again, the bird was still there, with feathers shining in the sunrise. It was such a beautiful sight that she walked towards the window with a smile on her face. 'I have come for you,' the bird said.

'For me? Who sent you?'

'No one! I am only allowed to come once a year and save a prisoner from Siahbar.'

'To save prisoners from Siahbar? I did not think that it was possible.'

'Let's just say that I have some unfinished business myself with Siahbar.'

'Why has she not been able to stop you or prevent your good deeds?' asked Suri, thinking that it must be another carefully planned trap by Siahbar.

'There are limitations to what I can achieve—and believe me when I say that she has tried to prevent me from coming. Once a year is all that I can do.'

Suri thought that she had nothing to lose by trusting the bird, as she was already suffering. 'We will come with you,' she said after a moment.

'Listen carefully, as there are terms and conditions—and I am still not sure whether I can take you or not,' the bird said, then continued: 'Siahbar can not reach you where I would take you, but she will do her best to follow me and stop us from reaching safety. When we are in the safety zone, she would not be able to harm you.

'Last but not least, you will have to feed me on the way. I need fuel and energy, as it is a long way. I feed on dried and salted meat.' Suri remembered the old lady's pack. She took it out of her pocket and showed the bird. 'You have been taught well. This pack is all you need,' said the bird with a pleased voice.

Suri helped Arsalan up and put him on the bird's back, and noticed how weak she had become. 'What are you doing?' asked the bird. 'I can only take you!'

Suri sank to the floor. 'You might as well leave, because I will not leave him here.'

The bird, overcome by feelings of loyalty and love, said, 'Well, you don't seem very heavy and neither does he, so perhaps, this time I can make an exception.'

Suri remembered the old lady's advice about keeping thin and smiled as she helped Arsalan on the bird's back. She jumped up and whispered that she was ready to fly.

Away they flew, and it was the best experience Suri had ever had. She whispered all the things that she was seeing and experiencing into Arsalan's ear hoping, that he might hear her.

After awhile, she started to feed the bird small pieces of meat, thinking that it had to last them the whole journey and the bird kept asking for more.

'I can sense Siahbar,' the bird suddenly said. "I can usually sense her from miles away. You need to be on guard.'

Suri tried her best to remain alert, and it wasn't long before she noticed a black bird flying towards them with Siahbar on its back. She informed the bird.

'Open your pack and throw one of the objects given to you by Sefidbar.' Suri realised it was the first time that she had heard the old woman's name. She opened her pack and threw the magic comb, and suddenly tall, dark trees grew behind them and surrounded Siahbar and her bird. Suri could not believe her eyes.

'Who exactly is Sefidbar?' she asked the bird.

'Sefidbar is Siahbar's twin sister. She is against all that Siahbar does, and believes her to be evil.' The bird asked for more meat and flew non-stop. Before long she warned Suri of Siahbar's presence again.

Suri looked down and discovered that Siahbar was riding on a horse below them. She took the jar of salted water and poured it down. The water turned into a sea and stopped Siahbar from riding after them. Suri was amazed at the magic that she had been given. But she understood now why the old woman knew so much about Siahbar.

She kept feeding the bird, knowing that there wasn't much left of the dried meat. 'Are we almost there?' Suri asked with worry in her voice.

'Are we running out of fuel?' asked the bird.

'There is still some left.'

'And we still have a way to go.'

After a while, the bird warned Suri of Siahbar's presence again. This time Siahbar was riding on a wild boar, riding as fast as ever. She quickly threw the last protection in her pack—the magic mirror. To her astonishment, the mirror turned into a mountain, as slippery as mirrors. Suri could see how Siahbar was struggling to climb the mountain, without success.

'We are almost there,' said the bird. 'Give me one last piece of meat.'

Suri looked in her pack and found no more meat. They had run out! 'I have no more left,' she said with desperation in her voice.

'I have to eat—otherwise I land.'

'Well, what else can I feed you?' Suri asked.

'Raw, fresh meat will have to do,' the bird responded. As Suri prepared herself to cut a small piece of her own body to use as food, she heard the bird say: 'Cut a piece of my thigh and feed it to me. I will heal in good time.'

Suri hesitated, then complied. Tears formed in her eyes for the bird's kindness.

Finally they landed well and unharmed in the land of safety and peace, and slowly Arsalan came to life. Siahbar's curses and weapons were disarmed in this safe place. The bird's thigh healed quickly enough and flew back to report to Sefid-bar about the happy ending of their story.

Suri and Arsalan made a good home in the land far away from evil and lived happily ever after."

11

The day was finally here—my dad was coming home!

The day could not pass quickly enough at school—a long day filled with lessons, breaks, and boring lectures. Not even friends who had smuggled in Michael Jackson photos and videos such as *Grease 2* and *Rambo* to share interested me much today, but I decided to have a look at the latest photos of Michael Jackson's "Thriller" anyway.

All of a sudden I heard a voice behind me. "Amani!" It was Khanom Nazemi.

"Yes, Miss," I said while discretely putting the forbidden photos in my pocket before turning around.

"I heard your father is coming home today."

"Yes," I said with a sigh of relief.

"You must be having a big celebration this evening."

"Only close family," I said, then, saved by the bell, I excused myself and ran inside.

Whew, that was close, I thought. For the rest of the day I kept myself to myself and counted down the hours.

I didn't know who to expect while waiting for my ride, but deep down I wished for my dad, and when I saw my grandfather I held my breath. "Don't fear!" he said. "Your father is home, but he is very tired, so I decided to come for you today."

I kept silent on the drive home. My grandfather wasn't much of talker, so it suited both of us to sit quietly on the fifteen-minute journey home.

When we got there, I ran upstairs, and Maman bozorg opened the door. She silently signalled me to be quiet. "He is resting. He was very tired."

"How long is he going to rest? Has Shahin seen him? Is Mum home?

"Why don't you attend to your homework and let him rest until dinnertime? We'll get together then."

"What about the party?" I asked.

"It was postponed! We will have it on Thursday."

I felt that something was not right, but I decided to retreat to my room and keep my anxieties to myself. I sat at my desk with opened books and tried to concentrate, but the hours passed so slowly and my concentration was affected by my worries. I went to the kitchen, opened the fridge door without knowing what I was looking for, and closed it again.

I went downstairs and knocked on my grandparent's door. Meme opened the door, hugged me, and asked me if I wanted some hot chocolate. I nodded.

Dipping biscuits in my drink, my tears poured down.

"You should be happy—your father is home."

"Have you seen him?" I managed to ask between the sobs.

"What do you mean?"

"Have you actually seen him? So you know that he has actually returned?" She nodded. "Is he well? Is he in one piece?" I asked, thankful that my questions were being answered.

"How you worry over nothing," she said. "Of course he is in one piece. He has lost weight and needs to gain his strength and get his energy back. We will see to that! In a couple of days he will be his old self and he can enjoy his homecoming celebration."

Feeling relieved, I finished my drink, hugged Meme, and asked to be excused to attend to my homework. Just before leaving, I thought I heard Shahin in the garden. I went to one of the bedrooms to see what all the laughter and singing was about, and I saw him on a yellow sporty bicycle, cycling in the garden.

"Is that yours?" I asked.

He ignored my question and seemed to be too preoccupied with his childhood glory. Then he finally said, "It is from Dad. He brought it back for me from his trip. It is a *soghatee*"—gift.

This is another painful custom that Iranians still obey. You are expected to bring back a gift from your trip for each member of your family, no matter how big or small a gift, to say that you have been thinking of them while you were away and that you love them.

It made me wonder what he had brought back for me, and I rushed out of the bedroom to the hallway when I heard my dad in the family room. "What is there to say? What can I tell you? Where can I start?"

"Rostam Jaan," my father's amoo said, "you need to tell us and let some of it out. It is not good for you to keep it inside."

My curiosity kicked in and I decided to hide behind the hallway door as no one had noticed my presence yet.

"Is it really as bad as they make it out to be on television?" my amoo asked.

"It is worse! Young children, as young as Shahin—may he be protected—walking on mine fields, people losing their loved ones, belongings, and body parts. There is not enough medication and medical support for the injured. You can't sleep as you hear constant cries and sobbing because of all the pain.

"There isn't enough morphine in the world to numb a child's pain from the loss of his leg or arms. One day you see them playing in the playground, and the next day you have them on your hospital bed with one leg in their hands, asking you to put it back and fix it.

"The bastard Saddam Hussein has ordered dolls with hidden explosives to be dropped on the playgrounds. The children play with the dolls and are blown to pieces. He is specifically targeting the children now."

"Rostam Jaan, you need to forget about all that," Meme said with a cry in her voice. It was obvious that she could not bear to hear anymore.

"Modar Jaan,"—Mother Dear—"how can I stop hearing the cries for help, the screams of pain, the children begging me to take them to safety? How can I forget a mother's appeal to have a look at the pieces of her son's body, to see if there is anything that we can do? How can I forget the father's pain from his loss, which has driven him insane? People's reactions, rooted in powerlessness, became too overwhelming to observe."

Meme wanted to seem brave for her son but couldn't bear to hear the rest. Instead she offered him encouragement for being so brave and having survived it.

My Babee proudly offered his advice of taking Valium for sleepless nights. Meanwhile, my amoo suggested therapy, and my father's amoo became very angry with the war and the system, which was followed by a political discussion. Soon everyone was talking over each other and forgot about my father, who was sitting in the middle of it all with his face down, shaking his head.

I wanted to rush over and hug him. I wanted to tell him how much we had missed him and how glad we were that he was home. I wanted to allow myself to be selfish, focus on my family, and tell him how glad I was that he had survived it all. I wanted to share my joy that I was not one of those fatherless children on television who bravely say that they are proud that their fathers died in a good cause as a martyr for their country.

"Shahla is expecting us for dinner," I heard my dad say, interrupting the discussion. "Shall we go upstairs for a delicious home-cooked meal? I sure have missed her cooking." It was interesting how my dad's way of leading the discussion and turning the focus to normality calmed everyone down, and how they all became one in their views over food, cooking, and home-cooked meals.

As soon as they all left and I could hear them upstairs, I sank onto the sofa and sobbed. I cried, thinking of the children, of the mothers and fathers in such hopeless situations. I cried happy tears for having my father back well and safe, and then I cried feeling guilty for having him back, as there were so many children who had lost their fathers.

When I opened the door, all the faces turned to me, each of them asking where I had been. "I was in the garden looking at Shahin's new bicycle," I lied with my head down.

"I know what this is about," my father said, hugging me. I have a *soghatee* for you too." I didn't want to let go, so he asked my mother to bring my package.

"Don't you want to open it?" my father asked, trying to release himself from my arms. "It may not be a bicycle, but believe me when I say that it will make you happy."

Trying to seem interested, I opened the package, and when I saw the Michael Jackson look-alike outfit from "Thriller," the red and black leather jacket with the leather trousers, gloves, and the shiny socks that I had been nagging about since my father had left, I burst in to tears.

I knew there were no Michael Jackson outfits where he had been. Where he was, children and families were struggling to survive and to stay alive. At that moment, Shahin's laughter and cheerfulness made me envy his lack of awareness.

"What is troubling you? I thought you would like it," my dad said.

"She does—she is just overwhelmed," my mum said, saving me with those words.

Just before bedtime, my father said, "I need to visit the family of a friend of mine tomorrow. I promised him that I would do so as soon as I returned to Tehran."

"I want to come," I said.

"I don't think you should."

"But I want to," I insisted, not knowing what I was getting myself into.

"We will all go with you, Rostam Jaan," my mother said.

12

In the car, as we were listening to Shahin's audio tapes, my mind wandered. I wondered whether my mum had heard my dad's stories, and how difficult it must be for them to keep it together.

My dad stopped the car and bought a cake on the way, and it smelled of fresh cream and fruit, which made me hungry. "It is rude to visit someone empty-handed," he used to say, and he liked to follow the customs.

I leaned on my Maman bozorg to rest and fell asleep, until I was woken up by my mother. "We are here, Shirin."

I watched my father go to the door, introduce himself, and make a *tarof* about not wanting to intrude. Soon enough he was convinced it was okay to visit, and we all followed.

Inside he handed the lady the cake, and she showed us the way to the living room. When she came back from the kitchen with teas on a silver tray, she asked if Shahin and I wanted to play with Ali. "Ali Jaan? You have company."

Ali was a lively, polite young man, same age as me, who seemed very enthusiastic about offering his company and sharing his toys. I told him about my cousin Ashkan, and how much he reminded me of him.

"My mother is his ammeh, and she loves him to bits, to the point that I sometimes get jealous," I said

"My ammeh loves me too. She is all the family that I have left," he said while showing Shahin his art-and-craft toolkit.

"What do you mean?" I asked.

"My mother passed away of cancer two years ago, when I was very young, and not long ago we heard that my father had become a martyr in the war."

I didn't know where to begin as I tried to digest this. I felt that it was a bit too overwhelming for me—I had just about recovered from yesterday and could not cope with any more.

"What is cancer?" Shahin asked.

"Shahin! I will tell you later," I said with a sharp voice, thinking that I really am not brave enough to hear about this.

"It's okay. People ask me that all the time," Ali said with a gentle voice. "It is an illness that there is no cure for. She fell ill and it took the doctors awhile to diagnose her illness, and when they finally diagnosed it, it was too late."

"Do you miss her?" Shahin asked.

"Shahin! Stop asking silly questions," I said, more sharply than before.

"It is just that I don't think that I could live without my mum," Shahin said, shaking his head.

I looked away to wipe my tears, then faced Ali and said, "You have to excuse Shahin—he is just a child and says as he feels."

"He is right, though," Ali said. "I never would have believed that I could live without my mother until I had to. I have younger siblings, and I had to stay strong for them, Ali said." He was very understanding of Shahin's way of thinking.

I had a sob stuck in my throat, and could barely think, never mind speak. "When did you hear about your father?" Shahin asked.

I might as well give up on Shahin, I thought.

"About two weeks ago. His hospital base was hit. I wasn't the only one losing a parent, but losing him meant that I became an orphan."

"Is that why you all wear black?" Shahin asked. I couldn't hold back my tears any longer.

Just then Ali's four-year-old sister walked in to bring us some cake.

§§§§§

"Baba! Next time we shouldn't take Shirin to any social gatherings. She embarrasses the whole family with her crying and sobbing. Ali had to put aside his own grief to comfort her in the end," Shahin said later in the car.

"*I* embarrass us? You are embarrassing *me* with your silly questions and intrusions."

"Stop it, you two," my mother said. "It was an emotional visit for all of us."

At home I brushed my teeth and went straight to my bedroom. Moments later I recognised my Maman bozorg's knocking, and without hesitation she walked in and sat next to me on the bed. "Tell me, Shirin Jaan—what is troubling you?"

"I don't know," I said. "I guess I am just feeling a bit overwhelmed." I pulled the cover up to hide half of my face, pretending that I wanted to go to sleep.

"Have I ever told you about the king with horns?"

I poked my face out and shook my head.

> The King had two tiny horns—one on each side of his head—but he had learned to live with them as long as he remembered to keep them a secret. He had realised that it would be an embarrassment and bring shame on him if his horns were discovered and talked about. Instead of something unique, he saw them as a weakness.
>
> 'If people found out, they would make you a laughing stock. You need to make sure that no one finds out,' his mother had said on her deathbed.
>
> Since she was the only one who had ever been allowed to cut his hair, he had to come up with a quick solution after she'd passed away. His first attempt to cut his own hair proved to be a disaster, and he thought that if the horns did not make him a laughing stock, then his newly cut hair would, so he called in a barber.
>
> The King's main condition for a contract was confidentiality—the barber had to swear that he would never reveal what he was about to see. But as soon as he removed the crown from the King's head and saw the two small horns sticking out, he started laughing and could not stop until he was out of breath. This made the King very uneasy, and reminded him of his mother's words.
>
> When the barber finally stopped laughing, he said, 'Wait until my wife hears about this. She is so fond of you.' The King could not bear the thought of anyone else knowing his secret, so he challenged the barber to a duel. Naturally the King won the battle and took the barber's life.
>
> The King began to wonder who he could trust, and after experiencing the same problem with other barbers, he

thought that perhaps humans were not capable of keeping secrets. His own destiny saddened him.

One day, as he looked in the mirror and saw that it was time to call in a barber, he felt tearful.

By the time the latest barber joined him in the bedroom, the King had already had his sword sharpened and polished. However, when the confidentiality agreement was discussed, this barber seemed to have a clear understanding of what was involved. He reassured the King that he had dealt with major cases of hair problems and diseases during his career, and he had learned to keep secrets.

The King removed his crown and focused on the barber's facial expression, expecting to catch him in sniggering or laughing. But instead all he saw was a concerned barber, who said, 'This secret must have been difficult for you to keep.' His empathy warmed the King's heart.

The barber decided to keep some of the King's hair longer to conceal the horns, in case he wanted to take his crown off. The barber worked hours on the hair—and finally when the King was shown the mirror, he smiled for the first time when he looked at himself. He could not see the horns, as they were very well hidden, and he could finally focus on his other facial features—his big hazel eyes and long dark eyelashes—and for the first time he saw himself as a handsome young man.

He was grateful to the barber and decided to spare his life. 'If you tell anybody, I will have to kill you, as well as anyone you have told. You must carry this secret of mine to your grave!' With those words of warning, the barber was allowed to leave.

Confident that he could keep the secret, the barber left the castle. At home he was asked by his wife to tell her about his day and he told her about the castle and described its beauty, but he said nothing about the King's secret.

As the days passed, the barber found it more and more difficult not to think about the King's horns. After all, this was the biggest secret that he had ever sworn to keep.

It gradually became more and more difficult for him to keep from blurting out the King's secret, and even his nights were plagued with thoughts of the horns—so much so that he lost sleep over them. The resulting loss of sleep left him tired and lacking energy, and soon his business and private life started to suffer. His failing energy, more apparent every day, robbed him of joy. His guilt over not being able to shoulder this huge burden created even more pressure for him.

He finally decided to discuss this matter with his wise father. 'Father,' he began, 'a few weeks ago I took an oath and promised to keep someone's secret. I find it to be terrible burden and it is affecting my life and well-being. I feel that I am changing, and not for the better.'

'Well, Son, this is a learning experience for you—never walk into unknown territories and make promises unless you know that you can keep them. You have to tell someone of this secret and release yourself, or it will eat you from within.'

'But if I reveal the secret, I will die, and I will be responsible for the safety of the person I told as well.'

'I see,' said his father. 'In that case, find your own way of releasing the secret that has become so poisonous inside you. Find a *thing* to tell it to—a stone, perhaps.'

The barber left his father, pondering what he had suggested. The more he thought about it, the more it made sense. An object could not disclose a secret, and it would be safe to tell it. The thought of another sleepless night made him even more determined to look for something to reveal the secret to.

The barber decided to rest while he was thinking of a plan and, looking around for a place to relax, he saw a well. He looked it over and saw that it had been abandoned and dry for years. Without hesitation, he put his head inside the well and yelled with all the energy he could muster: 'The King has two tiny horns on his head.'

He repeated this over and over again until he felt empty. This action left him more relieved and alive than he had imagined it would. It reminded him of when he was a child and had to digest a heavy meal. It had made him sick, tired, and lethargic. As soon as he'd vomited and emptied his belly of what had disagreed with him, he'd felt much better.

The barber went home to his loving family, which had patiently awaited his return. He remained the King's personal barber for many years because the King felt that he had found someone with whom he could share the secret—someone who was not frightened or disgusted."

I thought about my father and what his amoo had suggested: "You need to share your experience with someone, Rostam Jaan."

"Maman bozorg, I think Dad needs to discuss his experience with someone."

"I think that you are right. But let's leave that to your parents. As far as I can tell, they are dealing with it the best way that suits the whole family."

"You know that Ali had lost his mother to cancer, and his father in the war? In the same attack that we thought we'd lost my father?

"I know," my grandmother said, shaking her head. "You never think that it can happen to you until it does."

"What's going to happen to Ali? How can someone survive without parents? How will he cope?"

"I talk from experience when I say that you gain strength in mysterious ways when you need it the most. I lost my mother when I was six. I vaguely remember her beauty and her beautiful eyes, but I do remember her smile very clearly, especially when she was trying to hide her illness and her constant coughs. She had a very mild voice and a gentle attitude. My older sister had already settled down with the love of her life and had a happy home. Me and my brother, who was only a few years older than me, were told on the same day by my father that our mother had passed away.

"I wanted to see my mother and ask her why she had left us, but I wasn't allowed. They told me that there would be no point in asking her as she would not be able to answer, and I would only be disappointed.

"My brother understood as little as I did, but everyone noticed how much I struggled. I didn't understand why she had left us. I didn't know where she had gone, and I wanted to go with her. My father explained as best as he possibly could, but I was still confused.

"I wasn't allowed to attend the funeral as 'it would only upset the children,' I was told. A few days later, my father cleared the house of Mum's belongings, thinking it would be for the best.

"I managed to get a hold of her slippers and hide them under my bed. The next day when my dad went to work, I found the way to the cemetery. It took me awhile to find her grave, and when I finally did, I sat down and cried with her slippers in my arms. I asked her why she had left us and asked her to come back, or take me with her.

"I strictly followed my new ritual of spending time with my mother. Each morning I would wait until my father left for work and my brother went to school. Then I would dig out her slippers from under the bed and make my way to the graveyard. I would sit by her grave, cry, and ask her to take me with her, and by afternoon I would give up and go home for dinner.

"On the sixth day, while I was sobbing, pleading, and begging her to take me with her, I fell asleep on the stone, out of exhaustion. In my dream I saw my mother, who angrily took her slippers from me and told me to go away and leave her alone. She yelled so loud that I can still hear her say to let her go and get on with my life. I woke up shaking from fear, but I understood that it was time to let go.

"My father never remarried because he believed that a stepmother would not be suitable to raise us. He worked until late afternoon, and in the evenings he would come home and cook dinner for us and tuck us in and tell us one story per night. That is how I was able to sleep again.

"I could barely wait for story time. I would finish my dinner, anticipating a story that would take me into the mysterious world of Deeves, witches, angels, helping hands, *lohes*, good and evil and magic. It turned my focus away from my grief—even if it was only for a couple of hours a day.

"I can still hear my father when I tell these folk tales. It was my inheritance, and will be yours when you have children and grandchildren."

"I wonder if Ali's ammeh knows any folk tales that she can tell him," I said.

"We all have our own way of grieving. The young gentleman I saw today will find his own way soon enough, if he hasn't already. Sometimes people can find it patronising to have others grieve over their losses, the way you are for Ali. You are undermining his strength for surviving his loss only because you feel that you wouldn't have coped. It is not fair to Ali."

Those words were like cool water on burning fire and calmed me down, and in my next breath I could hear myself snore.

13

On the day of the celebration, I felt happy and confident to celebrate my dad's return. Most of the morning, Shahin and I helped by staying out of the way. Shahin sat with his Atari game in his room in front of the television. I went downstairs to help Meme choose her clothing for the evening. I loved the part when she would open her closet with all the dresses that she had kept over the years, carefully tucked away in the back.

I loved her turquoise-coloured lace suit that she said she had worn to my parent's wedding. She had stories to tell about each dress that she had worn to each party and celebration as the wife of a deputy bank manger. Then after all my pleading she would dig out the albums and show me photos of herself in the dresses, which sparked my imagination even more. I would ask for permission to try on her dresses and dream away while she made me Nesquik in the kitchen.

By the time I opened the door to our house to get myself dressed for the evening, the scent of different dishes, brewing and simmering away, the shapes of different cakes and pastries, the colourful fruit-plates and salads, were too tempting to resist a taste. This always left a trace and I was usually caught.

Soon the house was filled with laughter and smiles, my parents glowing as the guests of honours. I felt contained and happy. My father's uncles, aunts, and cousins were all gathered there, eating, laughing, singing, and taking photos to make the evening memorable—like any other ordinary family gathering, except we were celebrating not only my father's return but his life.

After dinner we all found a way to entertain, we told the latest jokes, and we showed off our new dancing, singing, or theatrical skills. Of course the curtains were fully drawn and we tried to keep it as low key as possible, because we were all aware of the new government's rules and regulations.

I loved spending time with my second cousins. Even though they were younger than me and some even younger than Shahin, I felt quite close to them and even over-protective sometimes. Shahin would share his games with them, and I would keep them entertained if they became bored.

Towards the end of the evening, I sat glued to Maman bozorg, knowing that she would leave in the morning.

While waiting for my dayee to pick her up, I remembered how impatiently I had been waiting and looking out of the window, expecting her over a month ago. *It is strange*, I thought, *how time passes quicker when you don't want it to*. I had been dreading this moment for so long that I felt quite relieved when I heard the buzzer. The torture of dreading the goodbye was finally over. It all flashed before my eyes, the days that we had spent together and her presence, which had made overcoming obstacles easier.

"I will miss you!" I whispered to her while saying goodbye.

"I will see you next Friday!" she whispered back. Every Friday we would visit Maman bozorg for lunch. That quick reminder made me smile.

§ § § § §

The following Friday was no ordinary Friday—it was Shabe Yalda. It is longest night of the year, which we celebrate in a special way. This obviously falls in December, and the weather can get very cold and frosty.

This year we decided to go to the family *bagh* (fruit garden) in Karaj to celebrate the Yalda. Karaj was only an hour drive from Tehran and, being in December, it was equally cold and frosty.

In the Land Rover, while listening to music, practising the latest dance moves with Ashkan and Shahin, and being told by Maman bozorg to keep it down, we started to plan for the evening and the Friday amongst ourselves. We were happy that we had left on Thursday afternoon and could have a sleepover in Karaj. That way we could take advantage of the whole Friday as well.

As soon as the car stopped, we ran towards the garden, pushed the gate open, and raced towards the small house, which was built in the middle of the *bagh*. It had two big rooms plus a kitchen and a bathroom. A lovely couple—Narges Khanom and Aghaye Bagheri—lived there to watch over the *bagh* and attend to its needs year-round.

As soon as we greeted Narges Khanom, we ran to the house to check if everything was in order. Boxes of fruits, pomegranates, melons, honeydews, and other seasonal fruits were laid out in the kitchen. Roasted nuts, such as pistachios, almonds, walnuts, and hazelnuts, were also set out for the evening snack. The grill was being set up by Aghaye Bagheri, the gardener, and the *kobideh* (minced meat) and *jojeh* (chicken) kebab skewers were on line, along with the colourful tomato skewers.

Soon Mum's cousins arrived one by one and parked their cars, and we all greeted each other with joy. We set up the volleyball net and started a match just before dark, while waiting for dinner. The aroma of freshly barbecued kebabs was torture, but the game had become too exciting to stop, so we played until it was too dark and too cold to feel our fingertips.

The *sofre* (table cloth) was already covered with kebabs, bread, and rice. Narges Khanom's own home-made *sir torshi*, (garlic pickle) added an extra treat to the meal.

It was on these rare occasions that we could sit around a *sofre* on the floor, and this made the evening even more pleasurable. During the meal we could hear the samovar bubbling away in the background, while listening to our fathers telling us stories about their childhood years and the games that they would invent to entertain themselves. We all laughed together at their silly inventions.

After clearing the *sofre*, we brought out decks of cards, backgammon and chess boards, and started the tournament. It was wonderful to see how these games brought everyone together no matter the age or gender. I was on the winning team, meaning that I was on Ashkan's team. We started with card games like *sheytoon* (the devil game) or *cheshmak* (the winking game) and finished with *Bibi Salam* (Hello Queen of Cards) and *Hokm* (Triumph).

When Narges Khanom and Mum announced the room was ready, we cheered for joy as the Yalda celebration was about to start. We greeted the room with astonishment. The *korsi* was the best of all traditions, one that we only kept if we were in the *bagh* in the middle of the winter. It was a big, low table with mini-heaters in the centre, covered with one, two, or more duvets or blankets, the thicker the covers, the better. We sat on the floor under the *korsi* in our favourite spots, wrapped in blankets, sipping tea, eating fruit, cracking nuts and seeds, and telling jokes and stories—and when our imaginations started to fail us, we sought support from poets such as Hafez.

I enjoyed most of the Iranian verses of Sadi, Khayam, and Rumi, but Hafez's poems seemed more meaningful and easier to understand for me. The Book of Hafez would be passed from one person to the next, each asking a question in their hearts and minds while opening the book. The poem would be the answer to the question. It was only for a laugh, some would say, but others religiously believed and swore by its powers and words of truth.

Because it was the longest night of the year, we could stay up as long as we wished. Some of us left for bed earlier than others, but we kept singing the hours away and listening to horror and ghost stories until we became too scared to leave our fort.

The next morning, we woke up to yet another sunny but frosty day in Karaj. Not to lose any time, after breakfast, the volleyball game and the badminton game started. Some of us went for a walk and some stayed indoors under the *korsi*, fearful of the cold outside.

For lunch every family had packed their own cold lunches: *salad aulovie* (chicken and potato salad), *kookoo sabzi* (spinach and herb burger) and *kookoo sibzamini* (potato burger), *dolmeh* (filled grape leaves), and a huge pot of *ashe reshte* (thick noodle soup) was simmering away. It was great to experience other people's cooking, whether to appreciate your own mum's cooking more or to learn from others, as some were creative and put in additional spices or ingredients that either made it unbearable or fascinating.

Before we knew it, it was time to say goodbye, and even though we all seemed to suffer from the Friday blues, still we felt energised and thankful for the Shabe Yalda celebrations and the opportunity for a family gathering.

14

The days did not pass as quickly now. It was dark and cold and snow had been predicted. We woke up every morning in anticipation of snow, but this year there seemed to be a delay in the usual seasonal weather process.

We were approaching the end of school term, which meant that the two weeks set aside for tests in different subjects were coming up. I was in year six, and I had already made my decision about my favourite subjects. Some I struggled with, like math and algebra, and some came easy to me—history and languages, for example. I felt that I was most attentive and popular in the classes where I enjoyed the subjects. I obviously had my favourite teachers, depending on the subjects they were teaching.

On one particularly boring day—not very different from any other recent day in one of my favourite classes, with one of my favourite teachers explaining the geographic location of northern Europe in her pleasing tone of voice and gentle way—an alarm sounded.

We sat still for a moment, almost as if we were in shock from the sound of the loudest alarm we had ever heard. For a moment we tried to figure out where it came from and what it was for. Then Khanom Nazeri opened the classroom door and yelled out: "What are you waiting for?"

"Is this the fire alarm?" Khanom Elahi asked.

"Fire alarm? I wish! The Iraqis are attacking! We must take refuge in the basement. It is the safest place to be right now!" Stricken with fear, and with all sorts of thoughts and emotions in our minds, we quickly lined up. Finally, Khanom Elahi opened the door—and I quickly wished that she hadn't.

The chaos was frightening and almost violent. The teachers wanted to calm the children down, but with a loud alarm ringing and younger children running in desperation in different directions, crying for their parents, and the older children running over them to the basement, the mission seemed quite impossible.

As the chaos continued, Khanom Elahi instructed us to remain orderly—even if we risked our own safety. We were based on the second floor, and in the queue we kept to the left and slowly walked down the stairs. Some were pushing others, falling down or running over each other. A war-zone atmosphere had definitely been created.

While trying to focus on other things to keep calm, I read the posters on the walls and one by one they made sense to me, for the first time. "You need to make the effort, and God will be there to support you in your aim to gain success."

Looking out of the window, I suddenly realised how much I loved our school. I remembered the change from the days when we sat in the classrooms with boys and played in the playground with them. How free and childish we had been allowed to be back then! English was my best subject, as I had been studying it since the age of four and felt confident in my English classes. Every Thursday we were taken to the cinema at the other end of the school for cartoons and Disney movies. Some Thursdays we had fancy dress parties and various other theme parties, which made it feel like we were attending school five days a week as to our usual six. In Iran you go to school six days a week, with Fridays off.

I was only six years old when Iran was turned upside down by the revolution, but I still remember the chaos. I remember how parents were queuing up at the gates to collect their children, confused and crying about the uncertainty of Iran's future.

I remember the days when home-made explosives and fires were set near our school, and people were marching in the middle of the streets, shouting "Allah o Akbar"—God is great—while stopping traffic. I even remembered having been stuck in the middle of the chaos with my mum one afternoon on our way home from school, when they had released tear gas. The following day there was a picture of it in the papers.

I remembered the day when we discovered a fence in the middle of the school playground, which was intended to separate the boys from the girls and we were told that we were no longer allowed to speak to or play with boys. The school café, with its famous milkshakes and hamburgers, closed down. Eventually the girls had to leave the school altogether and attend a so-called "girls' school." All English classes were ended, and instead of calling our teachers Ms. or Mrs., we had to call them *Khanom*. The teachers were responsible for informing us of daily changes in the school policies and procedures, even though they seemed confused themselves.

Then there was the business of the *hijab*, which was a long story itself—how we had to start covering our heads and hair. Soon a dress code for schools and offices was introduced, and we all found it extremely difficult. No music, dances, alcohol, or parties with boys or girls or watching videos were allowed—especially Hollywood movies. Women were not allowed to wear makeup, and men could not wear ties or short-sleeved shirts.

The big stores, such as Foroshgahe Korosh, has so little to offer these days. The first time we visited the store after the revolution, I felt tearful as I noticed that the makeup counters where my mum used to buy her Lancome mascara had closed down, and so had the hair and beauty sections where she had bought her Taft hair spray. The short skirts and western clothing had been removed. We had to wear trousers with dark *mantos* (long dresses), and cover our heads with *rosari* or *maghne*. When the revolution broke out, a lot of people emigrated and advised others to do the same. But so many families did not want to leave their homeland and relatives and hoped for the best. A year after the revolution, Saddam Hussein invaded Iran.

Sometimes I wished that I had not experienced life before the revolution. That way I wouldn't have known what life then had been like, and I wouldn't have missed it. Other days I feel privileged to have been a part of that life and experienced it, even if only for six years of my life. Of course I couldn't have an opinion about why the revolution happened, but it couldn't have been all roses if people of Iran risked their lives to revolt against the Shah's regime.

I'd been so preoccupied by my memories that I hardly noticed I was almost in the basement. I decided to use the toilet because I didn't know how long it would take for the all-clear alarm to be sounded. I had never seen the toilets this empty before, and I was quick. As I was making my way out, I heard a cry, which made me stop and look around. Behind one of the doors I found a little girl sitting with bloody tissues in her hands, covering her nose.

"What is your name?" I asked.

"Neda."

"Do you have a nosebleed?"

"It always happens when I get scared. Does it happen to you too?" she asked, expecting empathy.

"No, but it happens to my brother when he gets scared," I said. "My mum always says to put your head slightly back and stay calm, and before you know it, it will stop."

"I don't want to die," she cried out, which started the bleeding again.

"We are safe in the basement," I said calmly.

"I don't want my mum and dad to die." She looked at me as if she believed that I had a magic wand, which would keep them safe and make her wishes come true.

"I am sure that everyone has heard the city siren and are doing their best to stay safe," I said. "What you need to worry about is your own safety. They are probably counting on you to do that."

She stood up and, with one hand holding her nose with the tissues and the other holding my hand, we made our way to the basement. It was very crowded and we finally found a spot to sit. The sounds of bombings and planes were so scary, but worrying about Neda's fears had in a way diverted my attention from my own worries and fears of possible losses.

It was the longest hour of my life. As soon as the all clear was heard, chaos erupted as children wanted to get free and find out about their loved-ones' well-being and safety. I held on to Neda and asked her to stay calm. "We will have time enough to leave in peace," I said.

Parents were standing at the gates, greeting their children as if they had been returned to them for a second chance at life. The children, who were equally happy to see their parents, seemed extra happy with the various gifts promised to them.

Soon life returned to normality. I waited until Neda's father came for her and announced that they were all fine except her mother, who had developed a migraine.

The following day, I received a big bunch of flowers from Neda and her family as a thank-you, and I knew that I had made a friend for life.

15

Finally one morning our prayers were answered—snow! The radio announced that schools would be closed for the day. We cheered for joy, got dressed after breakfast, and headed to the garden to make snowmen and have a snowball fight.

Around lunch time, when we had made sure that every inch of snow had melted, we went inside for lunch. We had my mum's famous chicken sandwiches with gherkins, crawled under the duvet for a nap, and spent the afternoon watching videos and indulging in our laziness.

Every year we were blessed with a day or two of heavy snows in Tehran, when the schools would close. The powerless feeling of being stuck indoors was so rare that we enjoyed every minute of it. The lack of structure and disruption of our usual daily routine felt liberating. The confusion about tomorrow's lectures and classes prompted wishes for another day of snow. Stories about how badly traffic had been affected in Tehran, or how people struggled with the cold, or even how parents struggled to keep the children occupied, did not affect our wishes for a shorter school week.

The following day, as I was sitting fully clothed and ready for school, with one ear glued to the radio waiting for the announcements, I could hear my mum in the background. "Shirin Jaan! Don't keep your hopes up. Two days in a row is unheard of."

Even though I knew she was right, I was thinking, *One can always hope*. When I heard that the schools were closed again due to bad weather and the chaos from yesterday, I screamed for joy.

I was thinking of another day watching videos and playing video games, when my mum announced that she had prior plans and we had to join her for the day.

"But Mum," we protested.

"Don't 'but Mum' me. Not only are you going to have fun, but it will be an educational day for you."

As soon as we had turned to *Khiyabane* (street) Pahlavi, I sighed. "How educational will this be? We are going shopping, and it is good for us to learn how to make a bargain," I mocked.

"You are right—we are going shopping, and you will learn something new," she said patiently. With those words, she had caught my attention and my curiosity was set loose. I decided to be patient before I made further remarks.

And I kept quiet as we made our way in to the shoe shop Kafshe Meli. Nor did I say anything when my mum asked for assistance. "Aghaye Emami is expecting me," she said to the shop assistant.

"Shahla Khanom," we heard from behind the counter. "I have your order right here—it just arrived this morning," he said, pointing at the huge boxes piled up.

"Can I just have a quick look?" my mum asked.

"I like that! Even though we have been doing business for awhile, business is still business and these are hard times. You never know who you can trust."

I expected my mum to say that she trusts him and that it wasn't about him and simply make a *tarof*, as she usually does, but instead she went straight to the boxes, opened them, and looked inside. She took some of the boots out and examined them carefully. They seemed like simple brown-and-black boots with wool inside, in different sizes. Finally when she was through examining them, she asked, "How much do we owe you?"

"*Ghabel Nadare*, which is a *tarof*. It means that it is nothing and you don't need to pay."

"As you said, Aghaye Emami, this is business. Do I remember correctly when I say that we agreed on this amount?" She checked the figure with him.

"*Ey baba*! You can pay later! Really, *Ghabel Nadare*!"

"I would rather pay now, as I have the cash with me and I don't know when I will be coming this way again," she said, counting the money and giving it to him.

With the large boxes in the car and many questions swirling in my mind, I felt too numb to say anything or to ask any questions. After an hour's drive, we finally seemed to have arrived. We saw my dad on the pavement and became so excited that we jumped out of the car to greet him. I recognised my father's clinic, and soon the receptionist and his associates came down to greet us. I had only been there once before, but I found his workplace and the atmosphere very friendly.

Shahin was taken upstairs to the office and promised *sharbate leemoo* (lemonade). I insisted on staying downstairs with my parents, as I was curious about all the mystery hanging in the air today. I also felt that I had been cheated out of a part of our lives, which they had been leading in secret.

It was cold and my feet felt numb inside my boots, but I didn't complain in case I was sent inside. While standing in the cold, trying to keep warm and feeling self-absorbed, I noticed that a family came up to my father and thanked him for his kindness, collected two pair of boots in smaller sizes, blessed my parents for their generosity, and left.

When this routine was repeated more than twice, I felt warmer and more intrigued about it. People's smiles, gratitude, and faith in humankind made me want to be a part of it, and I did feel proud of having been part of it, even though I had only just found out about it.

All of the sudden, I remembered the Danish story about a poor girl who sold matches at Christmas as she walked past windows in the cold and wished she was a part of the celebrations inside, like everyone else. I think she froze to death by the end of the story.

When the unpacked boxes were empty, I pointed out that there were more boxes in the car. "Some of those we have promised to deliver personally," my father said.

For lunch my father insisted that we should try the *dizee* at a place around the corner from the clinic, which apparently made the best *dizee* in town. I hated the dish. I hated the smell and the texture of it, even though I had never dared to taste it.

It is a traditional dish made of lamb, chickpeas, potatoes, onions, white beans, and several spices. The dish was served in special *dizee* dishes, and we started with the soup, which tasted heavenly. When finished, we mashed the potatoes, lamb, chickpeas and the beans in the special dish that it was served in and enjoyed it with freshly baked bread and pickles on the side.

It was the best dish that I had ever tasted, and the whole experience was something that I would always treasure.

After tea and sweets, Shahin and I accompanied my parents on the promised delivery they had mentioned. Since it had been a long and a cold day, we fell asleep in the warm and cosy car.

"They are asleep! It is fine, honestly. We will come and visit another day," I heard my father say. I opened my eyes, sat up, and smiled, feeling energetic. I was looking forward to being invited in.

"I have a daughter your age," the gentleman said as he called for her. "Fatemeh Jaan, we have company."

He showed us the way through the school gates, and we followed him until we came to the basement of the school. He opened the door to a mid-sized room. On one side they had mattresses piled up. A small television was in the corner of the room, and a pregnant woman was under a blanket to keep warm. It looked like a prison cell with no windows—dark and very cold, even though I could see a gas heater in the middle of the room.

The pregnant woman greeted us with grace and went to the kitchen, which looked more like a cupboard, to make tea.

We sat on the floor and were served tea, and the adults started their own conversation. Fatemeh asked if we liked art and invited us to a corner where she showed us her paintings. She seemed very calm and sweet.

"Would you like me to give you my Atari?" Shahin asked out of the blue.

I could not believe that Shahin would offer something like that. He and his Atari were inseparable. He slept holding the joystick in his hands and played with it when he woke up. I was so touched by his gesture of kindness that I kissed his forehead. He immediately wiped it off, as he wasn't used to this kind of affection from me.

It had been a long day, but educational, as my mum had promised. In a way I was grateful to the snow and school being closed so I could discover and experience the secret part of our life that we had been living. I felt lucky, not only for what I had in life, but also for the parents that I had been blessed with. I only hoped that I could learn from their ways and follow their paths someday.

16

"Why could we not go with them?" Shahin cried.

"Because some places are not for children," Meme answered.

"It was a wedding! Believe me; children enjoy weddings more than adults do," I argued, equally disappointed.

"You were not invited! No children were allowed at that wedding," Meme said.

"Obviously there was an age limit, because you were not invited either," I said, annoyed.

"Actually, I was quite looking forward to spending the evening with you two," Meme said with a smile on her face.

We half-smiled back.

"Let's have some dinner first with your Babee, and then we can play whatever games you want to play."

We helped her setting the table, then putting out the salad, yoghurt dip, and pickles. She served the rice with a zucchini stew. As soon as I saw the colourless stew, I wanted to cry. I could see the lamb, zucchinis, and onions, but it lacked colour and it was the least tempting dish that she had ever made for us. Meme had a heart of gold and wished everyone well, but she was not known for her cooking skills.

I could not believe that here I was sitting at the dinner table, having zucchini stew with unscented rice, while at the wedding they were probably being offered at least seven different dishes, including desserts. The thought brought tears to my eyes, but the struggle with my own dilemma at the dinner table felt even sadder. I didn't want to seem ungrateful for the food and the effort that Meme had put into the meal, but at the same time I wanted to puke in private.

"So, Shirin Jaan—shall I serve it for you, or will you help yourself?" Meme asked, observing my facial expressions and movements.

I looked at Shahin's plate and saw that he had only asked for the lamb, and had left out the zucchinis. I hated meat so I wanted to leave that out, but the zucchinis looked boiled and overcooked. Instead I asked for the gravy of the stew.

"Let me give you some of the meat, onions, and zucchini," she said as she served me. I didn't protest because there would be no point, but I cried inside.

I played with my food while the adults talked about the weather, lack of oil, and the economy. I tried to hide my zucchini under the rice, passed the lamb to Shahin, and had some yoghurt with my rice.

"Shirin *Masti!*" my amoo called. *Mast* is yoghurt in Farsi, and because I loved yoghurt so much, my amoo gave me that nickname. I would have it with everything, and if there was no yoghurt at a meal, I would probably not eat.

While we were clearing the table, Shahin sat at the table and engaged in role-play with Amoo and Babee, pretending that he was the bank manager, giving out loans, cash, and coins. He had made his own paper money, as he was not allowed to use our Iropoloy money. It was fun to observe how soft or harsh he became in different circumstances, depending on the client's requests and attitudes. My Babee played it well with him, and his own experience allowed him to be playful with his role.

We managed to take Shahin upstairs just before eight so that he could brush his teeth and fall asleep in his own bed.

"So what do you want to do?" Meme asked. "Do you want to play a game?"

"Can you tell me a story?" I asked.

"I don't know any stories," she said.

"How come?" I asked, surprised.

"Let me think! I may know one or two stories."

I had brushed my teeth and was ready for bed, so I closed my eyes and waited for the sweet sounds:

> *Yeki bood, yeki nabood*—once upon a time there was a farmer who lived happily with his wife on a farm that he had inherited from his father, and his father from *his* father. He knew that he had to keep it in good condition as it was the family farm and one day would be passed on to his sons.
>
> The farmer's wife loved the sons but longed for a daughter as she had only been blessed with boys. Then the day came when the oldest son married a beautiful girl in town and blessed them with a granddaughter and a grandson.

> The farmer and his wife felt very blessed and would wait all week until the day when the grandchildren would come to visit.

When Meme paused, I asked, "What were the names of the grandchildren—Shirin and Shahin, by any chance?" I was trying to be cute. Meme burst into laughter.

Waiting patiently for her to finish laughing at her own trick, I asked, "Don't you really know any stories? With Deeves, *lohes*, and princes or…" She shook her head. "Didn't your mother tell you any stories?" I was determined to find out more.

"She passed away when I was three years old, and my father passed away shortly after."

"Oh, I am sorry, Meme Joon!" I said, feeling bad for asking. (*Joon* is an informal version of *jaan*, which means "dear.")

"Don't worry. Shall I tell you about your name story?" I had heard it a million times before, but I welcomed the idea with a satisfied nod. "When my mother Shirin passed away, may she rest in peace, we, the siblings, decided amongst ourselves to name our daughters 'Shirin' if we were ever blessed with one.

"I was blessed with two sons, but when you were born, I asked if we could name you Shirin. Your mother welcomed the idea, and only then did I tell her the story behind it. I didn't want her to name you out of an obligation to me or to my family.

"I held you like a daughter and loved you like one. You carry my mother's name, and I think that you carry it well. It is an ancient name, but it is still very popular."

"Isn't there a story about Shirin?" I asked, pretending I didn't know much about it.

"Yes—it goes like this," Meme said.

Farhad, the stonecutter, fell in love with Princess Shirin at first sight. The King promised Farhad the hand of his daughter in marriage if he would carve the stones on a mountain, which seemed very challenging and almost impossible. Farhad worked day and night to prove his undying love to the King for his daughter.

Many days later the news reached the King that Farhad had nearly accomplished his mission. This frightened the King, as he didn't want his daughter to marry a common stonecutter. The King consulted his *Vazeers*—Ministers—and together they laid out a detailed plan. They sent out a message to Farhad saying that Shirin had become ill and had passed away during the night.

Farhad had finished his work and stood proudly with his chisels in hand when he heard the news. He struck his head with the chisel and ended his own life, as he could not bear to live a day without Shirin.

As soon as she heard of Farhad's death, Shirin—who had been waiting patiently, naïvely believing her father's sincerity with his demand—rushed to where his body lay and struck her own head with the chisel too. Their two bodies were buried next to each other, in hope of love in the afterlife.

"There are obviously two versions of the story, but I only know this one," Meme said.

"It is okay, Meme Joon! It was lovely the way you told it." I hugged her, and in the next blink I dreamt of Shirin and Farhad and their undying love for each other.

17

Everyone was ill with the flu. Those who had not caught it were bound to get it and knew that they would any day now. There was no escape from it! Usually around this time of the year, with all the flu and bacteria going around, people tried to build up their immune systems with various recipes for different remedies in desperation.

It kept the women busy, the conversations of the day alive and exciting. But the households smelled vile. Because the remedies did not work, and people went from one recipe to another, the smells became worse.

Sometimes I didn't know which was worse—to go through a period of flu and get it over and done with, or taking the homemade remedies and living in fear of catching it. The worst part was when mothers or cooks tried to hide the taste of some notorious vegetable or herb with other ingredients, such as cheese, yoghurt, or lemon juice. There were also sad moments, when you weren't told about a hidden vegetable and found a slice of, say, turnip in your stew as a surprise—and the only consolation was that "It is good for you."

One day after class, as I was not looking forward to lunch at home, a classmate asked if I wanted to join them for some fried chicken at the fast-food restaurant around the corner. Excited about the idea, I asked my dad for permission when he came to pick me up, and surprisingly he agreed to come back later in the afternoon.

The last time I was in that restaurant, it was a KFC, and we had loved the takeaway buckets and the smell of fried chicken. Not much was changed inside, but the name had been removed. Even the scent of the frying oil, fries, and chicken reminded me of the past.

We ordered our meals with Pepsi, and the excitement of junk food, after being fed healthy food for weeks, was overwhelming. I ate with pleasure and licked my fingers cautiously, to avoid showing too much excitement, but when I was finished I craved more. We decided to order another meal to share between the four of us.

The conversation went from weather to food, and then to our teachers, school policies, and Michael Jackson. It was a lively discussion and everyone participated, their knowledge being tested on those subjects, but I noticed that my friend Shaparak had been mostly quiet.

"Is something the matter?" I asked her, interrupting a heated discussion between Leila and Nelly. All faces turned towards

Shaparak, and she became very uncomfortable at being the centre of the attention, so she just shook her head.

"Her mother was asked to wipe off her lipstick by the *Gasht*"—the hijab police—"with a tissue they had handed to her. When she did, she felt her lips burning and blood pouring down from her lips. The guards had hidden razor blades inside the tissues." Leila explained.

There was a long silence of shock! I felt embarrassed for making her uncomfortable and because I didn't know what to say. "Is she all right? Her lips, I mean," I finally asked.

"She will be, once it heals, but she has nightmares and can't sleep," Shaparak answered gently, having sensed my embarrassment.

"Are *you* all right?" I asked, concerned for my usually lively and bubbly friend.

Everyone fell silent. Then Leila said, "Shaparak was with her mother when it happened."

"I felt the blood drops on my cheeks," Shaparak said, swallowing her tears.

I didn't know what to say, but I couldn't contain my tears any longer. I felt sorry for my friend, who had witnessed an incident that had most probably scarred her for life. It could have so easily been me feeling my mum's blood drops on my cheeks. I thought about how often we were warned not to wear makeup and nail polish or to dress inappropriately. Not a single hair was to be shown, and tights under the *mantos* were not acceptable, as they do not cover the legs as they should. So we had to wear trousers under the *mantos*—even if we are just popping out to the corner shop for milk.

I was shaking, and the extra meal was cold and untouched. I just wanted to go home, and I was happy to see my father's face outside the window, gesturing for me to hop into the car. I hugged my friends and said that I was speechless.

"This must be the first time," Leila said, which made us laugh. The atmosphere became lighter, which made it easier to leave.

"Did you have a nice meal?" my father asked.

"The meal was nice," I answered.

"It must have been a nice change from all the healthy food you have been having at home."

I smiled. I wanted to tell him about Shaparak's mum. I wanted to tell him what I had heard, but I didn't want to ruin his day. Instead I said, "Thank you for allowing me the opportunity to have lunch with my friends today."

"I saw the excitement on your face and didn't want to deprive you of the chance. I had some errands to run anyway, and it suited me well to pick you up later."

When my dad opened the door, I couldn't smell any of the smell that I had been sniffing and living with for almost a month. In fact, there was no smell of any food. I went straight to the kitchen calling for my mum. There were no pots or any sign of food—in fact, no sign of anyone having eaten at home since breakfast.

"Dad, do you know where Mum is?"

"No," he said while looking through the mail. "Perhaps she was also fed up with all the healthy food and wanted to treat herself to some tasty junk food," he said jokingly and laughed.

I did not find the joke funny and started to search the house. Unsuccessful, I suggested that I go downstairs to ask Meme.

"Shirin Jaan, they will be home any minute—stop worrying," I heard my dad just before I shut the door.

"Meme, do you know where my mum is?" I asked, feeling breathless.

"No. Is she not home?"

I wanted to yell and say that if she was I wouldn't have asked her, but I remembered that my anger was not directed towards her. "Do you know where Shahin is?" I asked.

"He may be with your mum."

That much I figured myself, I thought. *But where is she?*

Not receiving the support that I needed in my search for Mum, I headed upstairs and tried to contain my fears by occupying myself with homework. I opened my book, but my concentration level was below zero. All I could see was Shaparak's face covered with drops of blood.

An hour later, I went to the living room where my father was speaking on the phone, with papers laid out in front of him.

"Was that Mum on the phone?"

"You know that it wasn't!"

"Where are they? Don't you care?" I realised how insensitive I sounded as soon as I said it.

"Shirin Jaan, they are probably stuck in traffic and will be home any minute," my father said, and obviously ignoring my insensitive comment.

I felt like a headless chicken, investigating each room for some evidence, and getting more and more desperate as it got darker outside. Finally I turned again to my father for a sympathetic ear. "I am really worried! This is not like Mum, and you know it. She usually leaves a note or lets Meme know if she has to pop out for something."

"But if she is stuck in traffic, there would be no way she could possibly let us know even if she wanted to. Tell me what worries you."

"I fear that she might be stopped by the *Gasht* for inappropriate dress. I fear that she might be harmed for wearing make up. I fear that they may hand her a razor covered in a tissue to wipe her makeup off, and she may cut herself. I fear that Shahin may witness all this and become…"

I ran and barely made it to the bathroom, where I threw up most of the chicken that I had been unable to digest, along with Shaparak's story. I washed my face, cried when I saw my pale face in the mirror, and washed it again.

My father was standing outside the bathroom door, waiting for me with the car keys in his hands. "If it worries you that much, we will go looking for them," he said, ready to turn the light off.

"But we don't know where they are, and we might also get stuck in traffic."

"The traffic should thin soon—and besides it would be better than sitting at home. Waiting itself can be a torture sometimes."

On the way down he suggested we tell Meme, in case they came home before us. I could hear the conversation through the open door. "But they may come home any time soon," Meme argued.

"Shirin is very upset over something and fears that Shahla may have been harmed. Her fear seems to be genuine, and I think that it would be best to look for them."

"Have you tried her mother's house?" Meme asked.

"No! That is a good idea. Shirin Jaan—do you want to call Maman bozorg?" my dad asked. I came in, but still stood very close to the door to make a point.

Then I heard my father saying my mother's name: "Shahla Jaan—where have you been?"

I sank to the floor. All the energy I had spent on fear, worry, and anger had left my body, and I fell like a sack of potatoes. Meme came to me and handed me a drink. "Here is some *Sharbat*. It is full of sugar."

Apparently my Maman bozorg had lost a distant family member, and when my mother heard about it, she left with Shahin to pay her respects and to comfort her in a difficult time.

When we reached Maman bozorg's house, I hugged my mum as never before. I examined her lips and stroked Shahin's head. I greeted the rest of the family members who had come to pay their respects.

Shahin, Ashkan, and I seized the opportunity to use the time for pleasure and left the adults to their mourning, and in the middle of the game I realised that I had already forgotten about my horrific day.

By the end of the evening, I could not believe that a day like this could end so well—my Maman bozorg agreed to spend a couple of days with us.

On the way back, I told everyone about Shaparak's mother. My father empathised, my mother apologised for worrying me, Shahin was asleep, and Maman bozorg held me tight.

"Did you say that you had fried chicken for lunch today?" I heard my mother ask before I fell asleep.

18

It was a most fulfilling experience to have my Maman bozorg stay, even if only for a couple of days. Just knowing that she would be there when we got home from school made it almost pleasurable leaving for school in the morning. I could even hear the birds singing—in winter!—and I didn't feel the cold during these cold days in Tehran. Even the honking of the traffic had a certain musical quality.

On the way home, I was daydreaming and looking ahead to the stories that I wanted to ask Maman bozorg to tell me, and my favourite meals that only she could make.

Well, little did I know of her own plans for the day. When I opened the kitchen door, I saw my mum and Maman bozorg unpacking packages of almonds, pistachios, hazelnuts, raisins, and roasted chickpeas, while Shahin was carefully examining them and once in a while sneaking one into his mouth.

"What is going on?" I asked.

"Maman bozorg had a *Moshkel gosha Nazr*," Mum said. I understood a *Nazr* to be a pact with a higher holy power, that if your wish came true you would perform a good deed. *Moshkel* meant "problem," and *gosha* meant "resolution," but it still didn't make sense to me as I stared at the mountains of nuts.

"What do you have to do? What does it mean, and what is the *Nazr* for?" I asked.

"You are not supposed to tell what your *Nazr* is for…"

"What is going on, Shahla?" my father interrupted.

"Maman has a *Moshkel gosha Nazr*, and we thought that we might as well do it here, as I haven't heard the story for a while."

"There is a story?" That got my attention, and my vote for going ahead.

"You know that I don't believe in this nonsense—and actually, neither do you," my father reminded her.

"It means a lot for her generation—and besides, there is no harm in it. There is a story that we might even enjoy, and the nuts are given away for charity."

"Starving families will surely appreciate a small pack of nuts in these difficult times," he said, leaving the kitchen.

Meme, who had also been invited to join, entered the kitchen with a big smile on her face, ready to play. I wanted to take part just for the story's sake, and the ritual's orderly process seemed fascinating.

Eight carefully washed hands, ready to start shelling and packing, started the race, to the sound of:

Yeki bood, yeki nabood—once up one a time there was a woodcutter, who lived happily with his daughter in a small cottage. Every morning at dawn he would make his way to the wilderness to collect dried bushes, which he sold in the city market to make a living. The father and daughter were grateful for the bread they shared each evening, bought with his daily earnings.

One evening, the woodcutter came home with a face full of shame and sorrow. He had to explain to his loving daughter that due to rain he hadn't been able to find enough sticks or dried bushes to sell, and therefore they had no bread for the evening meal.

His daughter, ever gracious, calmed him down and said that missing one evening meal wouldn't make any difference, and the hunger would make tomorrow's bread taste even better.

The following evening, the woodcutter again came home empty-handed and grief-stricken, saying that due to bad weather he was unable to sell what he had struggled to find during the day. He promised that he would do anything to bring food home for tomorrow's evening meal.

His daughter smiled and said that they would be able to survive two evenings without food.

On the third day, the woodcutter left earlier than usual and struggled again to find saleable wood, and once again he headed to the market, feeling hopeful. He sat for as long as he could, and when the sun finally set, he knew that the merchant's day had come to an end.

While packing his goods, he started to cry desperately. Even a piece of bread for his hungry daughter would be enough, he prayed.

Suddenly he noticed a rider on a white horse approaching him, asking him about his troubles. The woodcutter told the stranger of his three days of unpaid hard work and their hunger because of difficult times.

The handsome rider offered the woodcutter a pack of roasted chick peas and raisins and said, 'The *Moshkel Gosha*'—Remover of Difficulties—'has heard of your difficulties and is already helping you. If you want your good fortune to continue, you have to find someone in need once a month on a Friday evening and offer them a pack of nuts and raisins and tell the tale of *Moshkel Gosha*.'

When he got home, the woodcutter noticed a package outside his door, and when he opened it, he and his daughter found a loaf of date bread.

The following day, as his daughter was strolling on a broad path, a carriage stopped and a princess stepped down and asked if she wanted to become her handmaiden. The woodcutter's daughter accepted the amazing offer. Soon their days became brighter and more enjoyable as they used the gifts and presents from the princess to buy a nice house, and they became rich.

The woodcutter was unable to associate their good fortune with what the rider had told him. Perhaps believing the incident was an illusion caused by hunger and desperation, he conveniently forgot his promise to share and tell his tale to a person in need.

One day, when the princess went to swim in the lake of one of the King's private gardens, she took off her precious necklace and placed it on her clothes, which were guarded by her maid, the woodcutter's daughter.

Suddenly a big black bird flew by and snatched the necklace. The maid shouted and screamed at the bird, and the princess came to see what the shouting was about. When she heard the story, she immediately accused the woodcutter's daughter of stealing and lying.

The woodcutter was imprisoned as punishment for his daughter's actions. While sitting in the dark and cold prison one Friday evening, thinking of his life, he remembered his meeting with the young rider. He remembered his promise to him. He looked out of the tiny prison window and called to a beggar boy nearby.

The wood-cutter asked him to call his daughter and promised a prize for him. Then the woodcutter told his daughter to fetch him some nuts and raisins. He shared these with the boy and told him the tale, from the day of his days of hunger until the day of his fame and fortune.

The boy enjoyed the story and thanked him for the gift. Little did he know that his fortune was also about to change. After he left the woodcutter, a rich merchant approached him and held him, saying he had been stolen at birth. The gentleman explained that he recognised his son by the birthmark on his left cheek.

The following day, while the princess was having a swim in the lake, the bird returned with the necklace and placed it on her clothes. Witnessing the bird's actions, she felt ashamed and embarrassed for the trouble she had caused the woodcutter and his daughter. She ordered the woodcutter to be released and asked his daughter to return—not only as her handmaiden, but also as a loyal and trusting friend.

The woodcutter remembered his deed of charity every last Friday of the month, which continued their good fortune.

The pile of nuts, which had been carefully shelled and packed in small packages with red ribbons around their necks, looked beautiful and tempting. Maman bozorg handed us each a pack and prayed that good fortune would come to us.

I found the whole ritual fascinating and amusing. I had enjoyed the story and understood the concept, but I had many burning questions—which I decided to forget about, rather than risk ruining the moment. It was apparent that it meant a great deal to my Maman bozorg to perform this ritual—even if it meant nothing to me.

19

Even though the exam period was approaching and there was a lot of studying to do, I was happy to hear that we were going on a short trip for the weekend. My dad was going with a friend to visit an ill relative in a village in Mazandaran and asked if we wanted to go with him. For me the best part was that Maman bozorg, who was staying with us, would join us on the trip.

It was a four-hour journey, which we spent singing, listening to audio tapes, sleeping, and listening to my dad and his friends telling jokes.

"Almost there," Aghaye Majidi said, looking at us in the back seat. From there he directed my dad to turn onto a country road, along which we continued for another fifteen minutes or so.

Aghaye Majidi was a close friend of dad's, who also worked with him at the hospital. I knew him to be kind and have a good sense of humour.

I started to feel a bit uneasy when we finally approached the front door of the house. The village itself looked beautiful and matched the pictures that we had seen in books, magazines, or on television. The door looked heavy and yet opened easily with a touch. An old lady with a bent back greeted us at the door and said that she was expecting us.

How? I thought. *She doesn't have a phone or any form of communication device.*

In the middle of her garden, the biggest pot I had ever seen rested on a fire. We gathered around the open fire to keep warm. But she directed us to the front room for some tea and *koloche* (pastries typical of northern Iran).

It was cold and I was shaking, but from shock as well. I always welcomed the ideas of exploring new adventures, but this time I didn't know what to make of this experience.

In the front room, there was an Aladdin heater that was trying its best to produce heat, but failing as the wind kept blowing it out. The windows and the door to the room also failed to keep the cold out as the strong winds blew them open.

While the adults engaged in conversation and enjoyed their tea, Shahin and I found a corner and covered our feet with a blanket. "When do we go home?" Shahin asked me.

"Shush! They can hear you! It is rude to say that!" I whispered, fearing that they might have heard him.

"What is rude?" he asked me.

"To say that you want to go home. They may think that you are not enjoying their hospitality."

"But I am not!"

"I am not either, but I am not announcing it," I said with my teeth clenched together.

"If you support me in my protest, they may take us home."

"Don't be such a *sosool*"—snob. "One night of this won't kill you," I said, trying to sound older and wiser.

"But you yourself said that you didn't enjoy this either," he reminded me.

"If the living arrangements for the night here won't kill me, your comments surely will."

He started to read his comic book and I was left alone to sulk in my own misery. I felt like a snob. Why couldn't I find anything to entertain myself with? Why couldn't I see the beauty in what I was offered, as my mother had taught me? Why couldn't I enjoy this rare opportunity?

Just before dark, small gas lamps were lit and placed in the middle of the room, which made me realise that there was no electricity. I could not believe that I was experiencing how my forefathers had lived, which I had only been told about, and read about in history books.

The adults helped to serve the dinner. The aroma of the meal was too tempting to ignore. The *ash* (thick Iranian soup) was served with home-made cumin bread, dates, and feta cheese. *Ash* was not even one of my favourite meals, but I wasn't so spoiled that I wouldn't taste some.

It was hot and warmed me like nothing had until then, and it tasted like no other *ash* I had ever tasted before. Apparently the Mazandarian herbs and fresh lentils, chickpeas, and beans had worked their magic. The freshly made bread out of the wood-fired oven made the experience even more pleasurable. I had as many plates of soup as I could, until I was full.

"Tomorrow I will show you the lentil and chick pea plants," Aghaye Majidi said before we cleared the *sofre*.

Feeling a bit warmer after the dinner, I offered to help, collected the plates, and took them outside. I saw a girl my age there to help to the old lady, washing dishes in a bucket.

"What is your name?" I asked.

"Zahra," she replied.

"My name is Shirin," I said, not realising I was interrupting her work. "How old are you?"

"Twelve," she replied.

"You are my age," I said, pleased that I had guessed correctly. "Why don't you wash the dishes in the sink?"

"Which sink?" she asked without looking up.

I felt embarrassed at my own questions and assumption. She was right—not only was there no sink, but no running water. "Where do you get the water from?"

"From the well, and sometimes from the lake," she said, busy with the dishes.

"Is it very far? The well, I mean, or the lake."

"It depends what you mean by far," she said.

I knew that I was boring her with my questions, interrupting her work, and intruding into her space, so I asked if I could help with the dishes. She moved and allowed me some space to sit.

My bum froze from the cold, my hands became numb in the cold water, and my ears were being frozen by the wind. But I didn't complain, thinking if she could do it, so could I.

"Is this your first time here?" she finally asked.

"Is it that obvious?" I laughed at my own question.

"What is it like to live in the city?" she asked, ignoring my silly joke.

"I will tell you if you tell me what it is like to live here." Zahra nodded in agreement. "Well, you wash your dishes in a dishwashing machine or a sink. You keep your food in a fridge and sometimes in the freezer. You turn the lights on and off with switches, you have running water from faucets, and radiators provide heat."

Then it was her turn. "I started working at the age of nine. I was married off to my oldest cousin last year. I have never been to school and don't know any other way of living than this."

I thought long and hard about what to say, and the only thing I could come up with was, "You haven't missed much."

"Shirin, don't you want to use the bathroom?" I hadn't heard my mum ask me that question since I was about four. I looked at her in surprise. "It is just that we are going now, and if you want to you can come with us rather than go later on you own."

"I can finish here. Thank you for your company," Zahra said.

I was even more curious as my mum, holding a gas lamp, led my grandmother and Shahin into the dark towards the lavatory. In the dark we followed the weak light from the lamp to the lavatory. I opened the door and noticed the hole in the ground. It looked frightening. We took turns guarding the door.

"A red snake," Shahin shouted.

"Don't be ridiculous—snakes aren't red," I said, looking down to where he was pointing. Then I noticed a red thing crawling towards me. When I held the gas lamp closer, I saw a red and black snake approaching me, aiming for my feet. I screamed as loud as I could.

I heard Aghaye Majidi and my father running in the dark towards the sound of my scream, reassuring us that they would find us.

"These snakes are most harmless. They usually climb and hang from the trees. They are red and large, but quite harmless," Aghaye Majidi explained.

"Can I take one home, Dad?" Shahin asked.

Aghaye Majidi laughed and said, "They are not *that* harmless. Besides, they belong in the wild."

The sleeping arrangements had been planned well. Mattresses and pillows were all laid out by the time we had returned. The space of the room was used efficiently, and there were mattresses everywhere on the floor. While crawling underneath the duvet to keep warm, I felt I needed the comfort of a story from Maman bozorg.

"Will you tell us a story?" I asked.

"I don't think that it would be appropriate," she said. We are sharing the room with others, and I don't think that we should deprive them of their sleep. We should respect their privacy."

"I would like to hear a story too," Aghaye Majidi said.

"So would I," my father said.

When she realised that we all wanted to hear a story, she said, "Perhaps a short story then."

Yeki bood, yeki nabood—once upon a time there was a shopkeeper who was very arrogant, rich, and selfish. He always felt that he was the centre of the world, and sharing his wealth with others never crossed his mind.

He always moaned about his misfortune and misery to others—even to his wife and family. Never satisfied or pleased with what he had, he was greedy to have more.

One day he received a gift of roast chicken and a bottle of wine at his shop. He called for his clever servant and asked him to take it to his house. The shopkeeper dreamt of having the roast chicken with wine for lunch and, knowing how clever the servant was, he had to come up with a believable story.

'Listen to my instructions carefully,' he said. 'There is a live bird in this sack and bottle of poison. Do not open the bottle under any circumstances, as the smell may kill you. Do not open the sack as the bird might fly away.'

On the way home the young servant boy opened the sack and enjoyed the chicken while washing it down with excellent home-made wine.

The shop owner rushed home for lunch, dreaming of enjoying his lunch in secret, unwilling to share it with his family or friends.

At home he asked his wife where the sack was, and when he searched the house he didn't find it. He realised that the boy had not delivered the sack.

Angrily, he kicked and shouted at the boy when he found him lying under a tree, not far from home. 'Where is my sack?'

'Master, you will not believe this, but as soon as I left the shop, a strong wind blew the sack out of my hand and the bird flew away. I was so devastated to have disappointed you that I drank the poison, and now I am lying here, awaiting my death.'

The story was short and sweet, and everyone laughed. Soon everyone started to share their interesting short stories and experiences.

Just before sunrise the cold woke me. I was trying to find another cover when I suddenly heard a whisper: "Shirin Jaan—are you awake?"

"Maman bozorg, is that you?" I whispered back. She sounded wide awake, as if she hadn't slept a wink.

"I have been holding myself since I don't know when. I needed to go to that lavatory, but I didn't dare go in the dark. The oil lamps were out of oil, and with the snakes and the experience of visiting the lavatory last night, I couldn't go."

"What time is it?" I asked, as if I hadn't heard a word she said.

"Did you hear me? Will you come with me?" she asked.

"Let me put my jacket on," I said and, half asleep, I followed her into the cold. It was turning light and that made it easier to see.

The scene overlooking the hills and farms as the sun rose was amazing. I breathed in the fresh air and took mental pictures of the rare beauty that greeted me this morning. Little did I know that this was only the beginning of a beautiful sunny day as the cocks crowed and the hens laid eggs for breakfast. Later there would be a walk through the lentil and bean fields, a picnic at the lake, where we would watch the fish playing and jumping to show off their beautiful colours, and jars of fresh home-made quince jam to take home.

It was strange how I had adapted to country life in one day, and I found it difficult to say goodbye to Zahra and the old lady when the time came.

"She will be all right. She has been treated, given the correct dosage of medication, and she will be properly looked after," my father comforted me.

I knew that where she lived, with all the fresh air, beautiful scenery, fresh organic food, and help from Zahra, she would probably live for many years to come.

20

February, 1985—It was almost time for exams, and preparations consumed our days. The madness had begun! The panic in every household was predictable and contagious. The students were studying hard, staying up late and torturing themselves to prove that they were doing their best to please their parents. The parents were providing tutoring to their children—either themselves, or booking the most expensive private tutors available, to prove to their children and others that they were doing their best, "as responsible parents."

Recipes to provide the best nutrition and energy were exchanged between households. "Fish and lentils are good for the brain," was the motto of the month. Some would even take it to a higher power and ask for a blessing, for a prayer, or even make a *Nazr*.

And then there were the mind games, threats, or even bribes common in most households. "I will buy you this, if you pass your exams with a high grade," or, "I will kick your butt and feed you to the wild animals if you fail," or, "Your father will kill us both if you fail, for the shame that you have brought to the family."

The pressure was on and it was boiling under the lids. The exam period lasted for two weeks, and the anxiety continued until the results came back from the schools—which was another two weeks. It was a month of hell, but it was expected as it happened three times a year.

Just days before the first day of the exams, while I had locked myself in my bedroom to study, I heard a knock on my bedroom door. "May I came in?" I recognised my father's voice. He entered before I had a chance to reply. "Shirin Jaan—I don't want to take up much of your time, and I can see that you are very busy with your studies, but I think that it is best to talk now before I regret the whole thing."

I looked at him in confusion, and all sorts of thoughts went through my mind. Finally he said, "I have decided to send you away for awhile."

For a moment I thought that I hadn't heard him correctly. Then he went on: "As you know, it has become very unsafe to live in Tehran these days. City siren go off on a daily basis these days. The government advises us to evacuate Tehran, as Iraqi troops are getting closer. We hear every day on the news how someone has lost a family member or even their entire families in the attacks. It can happen, you know. It is not a joke. I have seen it happening with my own eyes." He avoided eye contact with me.

"Are you suggesting that I leave Tehran?" I asked.

"Not just Tehran—Iran," he said.

I could not believe my ears nor could I believe my father suggesting his child leaving home. "It's almost time for exams. I know that I will do well. I have studied hard!" I pleaded.

"Your life is more precious to me than any exams or grades…

"What kind of life would I have without my family?" I interrupted.

"Your mother and Shahin will go with you. I have to send you to safety, far away from here."

"What about you? What about Meme, Babee, Amoo, Maman bozorg, Ashkan, Dayee, Khale Shokouh, my cousins?"

"It will only be for a short while. You will come back, or they will come and visit you."

"I don't want to go!" I said, shaking my head.

"It was not an easy decision, believe me, but I need to consider your safety. Almost every night we have to evacuate our bedrooms and run down to the basement for safety. I don't like saying goodbye to you in the mornings when I am dropping you off at school, not knowing whether I will see you again in the afternoon. I cannot rest easily until you are safe."

There was a long pause before he stood and said, "Your mother and I have decided that we must act quickly, but there are no details to our plans yet. It has to be soon—that is all we know."

I knew that this was no time to argue. I needed time to digest all of this, so I decided to go to bed early. Had I done something wrong? Was this a punishment? If not, why does it feel like one? Why did it have to be soon?

§§§§§

Almost a month from today is Nowroz, the Iranian New Year, I thought. In the week before *Nowroz*—the equinox, or the beginning of spring—while the last of the snow is disappearing and the fresh breeze of spring is in the air, we do our spring cleaning.

The windows would be opened in every house and flat to let in the fresh air and let the dust out. The Persian rugs would be washed and hung to be beaten clean. Every drawer and cupboard would be searched, cleaned, dusted, and reorganised. The silver would be polished and the windows would be washed. Cleaning tips would be exchanged from house to house—how to remove the stain of tea in the kettle, or lime scale in the bathrooms, and so on. The house would smell so fresh that you want to keep it as clean forever.

On *Chahar Shanbe Souri*, the last Tuesday of the year, we would come home from school, feeling excited about the two weeks of holidays coming up in a few days.

We would start the evening by colouring and decorating boiled eggs, which would later be placed on the *Nowroz* table. We would treat ourselves to the special sweet nut mixture while decorating the eggs. The mixture usually contained dried figs, raisins, and dates, to sweeten the mixture of unsalted pistachios, almonds, hazelnuts, and walnuts.

The special sweets for the occasion, such as *baghlava* (baklava) and *gaz*—which is similar to nougat—and Turkish delight were served with tea, which filled the room with the aroma of rose water, cardamom, and saffron.

Towards evening the men would prepare three or more wood fires in the garden, while the women would put the final touches to the evening meal—*ashe reshte* (thick Iranian noodle soup). We would eagerly watch and impatiently wait in a queue to jump over the fire and sing, "*Zardie man az tou Sorkhie tou az man*"—we give our illnesses to you (the fire) and receive health from you.

After the meal, we would read poems and have them interpreted by the oldest member of the family while waiting for the best part of the evening—when a trick or treater would knock on the door. They would be masked and banging with a spoon against a bowl. We would offer them nuts and sweets, and figure out which family member was tricking us. It would be a family evening full of joy, noise, and cheers in every household in Iran!

There are many theories as to why we celebrate the night to the last Wednesday of the year in Iran. Some say that Wednesday was considered a cursed day in ancient Persian history—and it was hoped that if the *last* Wednesday of the year was celebrated, future Wednesdays would be luckier. Others believe that this tradition began to give thanks for the previous year's health and happiness, while exchanging any remaining paleness and sickness with the warmth and vibrancy of the fire. As for me, I say, "Let's just enjoy the celebrations, whatever the reasons may be."

Just days before we celebrate *Nowroz* and welcome the first day of spring with open arms, every household in Tehran searches finest, preferably red, *seeb* (apples), fresh *soumagh* (from sumac berries), freshly made *samanou* (a sweet pudding made from wheat), *serkeh* red grape vinegar, *seer* (big white garlic), seasonal *sonbol* (hyacinth), *senjed* (dried fruit of the jujube tree), *sabzeh* (wheat, barley or lentil sprouts growing in a dish), *sekkeh* (coins) in a small bowl of water, lit candles, a mirror, a holy book, the decorated eggs from *Chahar Shanbe Souri*, special *Nowroz* pastries such as chickpea sweets and sesame seed candy—and, least but not least, live goldfish in a bowl, swimming around and chasing each other.

Just hours before, the final touches are put to the *haft seen* (*Nowroz* table), and the radio or the television is turned on to hear the countdown to the new year. The smell of fried white fish and green herb and saffron rice stewing softly makes one forget the rest of the celebrations.

The usually heavily congested Tehran is on this day as empty of cars as the desert, though you may see someone running at the last minute to reach his family at home, or to look for a vital ingredient for the *haft seen*.

Just minutes before, the family gathers around the *haft seen*, all of us bathed, cleaned, and groomed, showing off our new clothes and waiting for the final countdown and the exact moment of the arrival of spring.

Finally, alerted by the sound of trumpet on the radio in the background, Iranians greet the *Nowroz*. At that moment, all Iranians are united, no matter what age, religion, or political view, and they all proudly celebrate the 2,500 year old tradition.

The celebrations start with children receiving gifts from their parents and extended family. They receive money, which they never ever see because it is usually put in a bank account. There are a lot of greetings, hugs, and kisses from young to old, and a lot of good food, sweets, seasonal fruits, and nuts are consumed while visiting the elders.

Then it is off to Shomal—northern Iran—for fresh spring breezes and two weeks of rest until *Sizde Bedar*, the thirteenth day of *Nowroz*. That is when the end of *Nowroz* is celebrated by picnicking or spending the day out with family. It is a day of celebrating nature.

Then comes the saddest afternoon of the year, when the celebrations end and everyone has to get home to prepare for school or work in the morning. Getting stuck in the *Sizde Bedar* traffic is a wake-up call to reality and a gentle reminder of a normal daily routine of life in Tehran.

§ § § § §

"Shirin, are you awake?" my mother whispered, waking me up from my daydream.

I nothing until she sat on my bed. "Why didn't you tell me about the plans? Why didn't you say anything sooner?" I complained, unable to contain my anger any longer.

"What was there to say? We have no specific plans yet, but your father wanted you to know before he made further plans."

"I don't want to go! I want to stay here with my family."

"It will only be for a short time. Believe me—I can't stay away from them too long either."

"Why can't we wait until after *Nowroz*?" I asked.

"Your father seems to believe that it will not be safe around that time. We have to move soon. Besides, who knows—we may be back before *Nowroz*, the war may be over by *Nowroz*," she said, trying to comfort me.

"Listen," she said with kiss while tucking me in, "you have been given a lot to think about for one evening. Why don't you focus on the good things, like the new world that you are about to explore, new people that you will meet, and the new language that you will learn?"

A new world, new people, new language—more scary than exciting, I thought as I closed my eyes to the night.

21

A few days later, when I had finally become comfortable with my denial and convinced myself that the conversation with my father may just have been a bad dream, Meme asked me to come down for her magical milkshake, to provide me with nutrition before my exams.

It took me a little longer than usual to interrupt my studying and make my way downstairs. Impatiently, I opened their front door and heard my father: "It is difficult for us all! I will miss them too. It will only be for a while."

"I cannot live without them," Meme cried.

"Those children you claim that you love so much live in constant fear," he said. "I live in constant fear of losing them…for good. At some point we have to stop being selfish and put their safety first."

"I know that you have their best interests at heart, and so do I, but I can not help it. I just can't see my days without them," she barely managed to say before she burst into tears again.

"We have to be strong so that we can convince them that this is a good idea. We cannot make them doubtful or fearful about this," my father said as he comforted her with half a hug.

My hope that my father's plans were just a bad dream were shattered into pieces. I started to cry silently as I realised that my own plan to "keep silent and it might just fade away a like a bad dream" had failed.

My father was determined, and all there was left for us to do was to start preparing and say our goodbyes. It was painful, more painful than waking up after my tonsil operation at the age of six, or when we heard that my father's uncle, a very sweet and gentle man, had passed away—and perhaps, even more painful than when I was asked by Meme to pray for my mother when had suffered an embolism during the caesarean birth of Shahin. "Little girl's prayers are heard," she said.

I wish God could hear me now, but perhaps he only listens to the little girls, and I am not little any more, I reasoned with myself. I didn't want any attention on me or my tears or my grief, so I forgot about the milkshake and went upstairs until I heard Meme call me two hours later.

We didn't have to use words to describe our grief—our eyes spoke clearly of it. It was an awkward silence, and I tried to keep busy with my milkshake. I wanted to make small, everyday, conversation, but simply couldn't. I wanted to say something about my exams and my feelings about them, but what would be the point? I didn't think that I would even be able to finish them before we had to leave.

What was even the point of the milkshake? I wanted to ask, but I swallowed the question along with the drink, which stuck in my throat halfway down.

"I comfort myself that it will only be for a short time, you know," my Meme said, finally breaking the silence.

"Why don't you come with us? I asked.

"You know I can't leave your amoo and Babee. Besides, we cannot all come with you. We will hold the fort until you come back."

"I don't want to go!" I cried.

"Shirin Jaan! These are difficult times for us all. You don't want to make it even more difficult, do you? Sometimes adults know better, and we just have to trust that."

"You are older than dad and you don't want us to leave. Perhaps you know better."

"I doubt it, Love! I don't think with my brain, I think with my heart when I say that I don't want you to go. I will have to learn to stay strong for you and you will have to do the same for me."

Suddenly, in the midst of my desperation and resistance, I had an idea. "What if we do a *Moshkel Gosha Nazr*? Do you remember when Maman bozorg did one last month? She said that her *Nazr* came through, and I know the story now, so all we need is a mixture of nuts—and we need to be at least two people in the process. I tell the story and you listen."

Meme laughed, the first time I heard her laugh today. "A *Moshkel Gosha Nazr* to stay in war zone? We should do the *Nazr* for your safety? You are missing the point!"

"No—*you* are missing the point. How can I live if not with my family in the country that I have been brought up in and know as my motherland? What if I never come back? What if I never see you again? What if abroad isn't safer than here? Don't people die in car accidents or other ways in safe countries? What if I die of heartache?"

I stopped when I heard Meme sobbing. I remembered what she had said about staying strong for her. "I will stay strong—I promise. Please don't cry," I pleaded!

Meme went to kitchen to grab some tissues. I followed and hugged her as hard as I could. "Just the thought of seeing you again one day will keep me alive," I said.

She hugged me back. "We have to stay positive and strong."

"I hear you, Meme Joon."

Before closing the door on my way upstairs, I heard her say, "Remind me to ask your father if there will be yoghurt there."

"Where?" I asked, thinking that I must have missed a part of the conversation.

"You know—abroad?"

"Why?" I asked, still feeling confused.

"I don't know if you will survive without yoghurt. You have to have yoghurt with everything you eat."

I will survive without yoghurt, but not without you, I whispered to myself in tears, before I closed the door behind me.

22

The days passed quickly and yet at the same time slowly—quickly because I knew we would leave soon and I didn't want to let go of the time. But they passed slowly because I wanted to celebrate *Nowroz* with my family in Iran, and *Nowroz* was still a month off. I didn't put much effort or energy into my studies or my exams. Every time we saw a family member or went out for dinner at Shater Abbas Restaurant or for ice cream at Ladan Bakery, I felt that it was for the last time. It was difficult to say goodbye to some more than others.

I was in denial for awhile before I felt that I needed to take the bull by the horns and say goodbye in my own way to Ashkan. Then we were both in denial until we figured that we were only fooling ourselves. After that we decided to take action, and we planned for him to come with us. We approached Dayee about it, but he refused immediately. After that, the grieving process started. It felt like saying goodbye to a twin, and that was when I realised that life without him was unimaginable.

Many times I started to write him a goodbye letter, but I ripped it up before finishing. Most of the letters started with; "You are the most loyal, honest, and considerate cousin, older brother, and friend that I have ever known." But then I thought, *How can you say goodbye to someone like him even if we would only be apart for a short time?* I spoke to him almost every day on the phone ever since I learned to hold it, and I saw him almost every Friday for twelve years. We had never been apart. We even dealt with our arguments without any involvement from our elders, which made making up even sweeter.

We were told that we had a falling out once, at the age three, over a bug that had flown in through the car window. Ashkan thought it was a mosquito, and I thought it was bee. We had been left to sort things out. Both of us had stuck to our theories—and till this day, if a family member asks "Was it a bee or a mosquito?" we stick to our own theory.

We were also overprotective of each other. No one would dare to harm, hurt, or say bad words about either of us. If he was hurt, I would hurt. I believed that having him in my life made me realise what sibling love truly meant.

Secretly I wished and prayed that my father would delay his plan till after Nowroz, until the day he called me and Shahin in the family room for a private chat, in the third week of February. He told us that we were leaving in three days, and that he wanted us to be strong and brave, and to behave well. He told us that he expected us to look after Mother, and that he counted on us as we were old enough to understand how to behave as adults if we needed to.

He turned to me and said that, as the oldest, he expected me to support my mother on the journey. He said Shahin had to be the man of the family until he joined us. "Have I ever told you what your name means, Shahin Jaan?" he asked, then without waiting for response, he explained: "Shahin means eagle. Your name was carefully chosen, as I wanted to have a strong, brave, and wise son in the family to support me when I wasn't there. Of course, it is also my favourite football team," he added with a wink.

I sat silently, my head filled with so many questions that I couldn't ask—*Where were we going? Why can't we wait until after Nowroz? Will I see Ashkan or Maman bozorg before we leave? How long are we going for? When will you join us? What can we take with us?*

"Do you have any questions?" My father asked, perhaps reading my mind.

"What about my braces?" I asked instead.

"What about them?"

"Doctor Javani said that I should visit him in three months for a check-up and further adjustments. I have an appointment with him in a month," I said pleadingly.

"Shirin Jaan, I will speak to Doctor Javani and find you a good doctor abroad. I promise!"

"Can I take my Walkman with me?" Shahin asked.

"No, but I promise to buy you a new one, and an Atari game, when you are safely abroad."

"What about our video?"

"Shahin Jaan, I need to keep myself entertained in the evenings, keep my mind busy so I won't feel your absence."

"*Chitty Chitty Bang Bang* is my favourite. I will leave the tape for you," Shahin said and hugged my father.

My father wiped his tears and said, "I know that this is the right decision, I know that I am doing right by you." He said it over and over again, as if trying to convince himself.

Just before leaving, he said, "Your Maman bozorg and Ashkan will be joining us for dinner and stay until your departure."

I was disappointed by my lack of joy over the news. It felt as if they were the last dinners we would ever have together. I couldn't deal with the pressure of planning for the last two days, so I decided to leave it to fate.

Greeting Maman bozorg and Ashkan was like greeting grieving family members, and when we gathered around the dining table for dinner, it definitely felt like an early funeral. It seemed like the end of an era, the loss of family gatherings, the loss of family belonging—losses that no one wanted to admit to or put into words, lest they become real.

When we were finally excused from the table, we managed to say a few words and make promises and pacts like, "We will have to write every day and speak on the phone as much as we can, never to forget each other, and no matter how long we have to wait we will live in the hope that we will have a reunion one day"—until we were interrupted by my Maman bozorg.

"I see that you have started without me," she said, and sat beside us on the bedroom carpet.

I couldn't even look her in the eyes. I couldn't say goodbye to her, not to Maman bozorg. How could I even begin to think about parting with her? She had been my mentor, teacher of life, wisdom, and patience. I felt dizzy and sick from all the overwhelming emotions.

To my surprise, I expressed my emotions in an unexpected way: "What do you care where we are going? Or how far we are going? You never cared for us anyway! It isn't as if you lived with us or we saw you every day! It would have much more difficult for you to separate from Ashkan, who you see every day. You didn't even try to stop us from going," I said with my voice raised.

"If I don't see you every day, I speak to you on the phone everyday. If I don't hear your voice on a daily basis, I suffer from heartache. Just because I am not voicing my pain doesn't mean that I am not in pain. My emotions don't count, as I am thinking of your safety," she said, and removed her eyeglasses to wipe her tears.

Shahin, Ashkan, and I fitted ourselves in her lap and covered her face with kisses. I felt embarrassed at my outburst, but somehow it had allowed me to feel affectionate again.

"These are difficult times for all of us—you, who are reluctant to leave your safety zone here in order find a new home in an unknown world, and us, who are reluctant to let go of you and feel abandoned in an unsafe part of the world. The grief and loss we all have to come to terms with, my child, are for each of us to deal with in our own unique ways," she said.

"Let me tell you this—I could never have wished for better grandchildren than you. I may not be able to come with you. But I will always be with you. You will never be rid of my voice, my tales, my teachings—and in this way, I will always be with you."

"Can you tell us a story?" Shahin pleaded.

"I promise that I will tell you one tomorrow. I promise that I will tell you one story that I haven't told any of you before. This evening I will dedicate to your parents. There are so many things to go through and so many things to say."

With that promise, we parted for the night and went to bed.

§§§§§

The morning began with phone calls, a lot of footsteps, loud voices—and even shouting from one room to another, hoping that the other would hear the message. I finally left my bedroom and joined the mayhem. It was difficult to avoid feeling the tension.

Only the essentials were supposed to be packed. There was no room for things that had sentimental value—in fact, nothing of value was to been taken. The departure was early following morning, before dawn.

The day was filled with goodbyes, hugs, and kisses with the immediate family, but the time limit and the packing left me no time to realise that I was actually departing.

When hunger struck by lunchtime, Meme rang the bell and entered with a big pot of casserole and rice. The family gathered around the dining table for lunch, and even though Mum said there still was much to do, we were afforded some time to focus on what we had done so far and what was left.

Later in the afternoon, it was decided that the children should watch a video to stay out of the way. We gladly accepted. One video turned into two, and by the time we knew it, sausage and fries were ordered from our favourite place around the corner.

With each of us holding onto a red takeaway box, ready to open and unravel the mystery of what it contained—as if we had no idea—we played a third video. With one eye on the television so as not to miss any scenes, and the other eye on the box that contained fries, two sausages, and ketchup, we started our mini-party for three.

Late evening, feeling that we couldn't keep our eyes open much longer, I looked for Maman bozorg in the kitchen. "Will you tell us the story now?" I asked with caution, knowing that they probably still had a lot to do.

"Haven't you had enough already, with all the videos you have been watching?" Mother asked.

"A promise is a promise," Maman bozorg said, standing up and following me to the bedroom.

Her place was already laid out so that we didn't have to argue about that in her presence and waste any time. The three of us, washed and brushed and ready for bed, just managed to crawl under the duvet before we heard:

> *Yeki bood, yeki nabood*—once upon a time there was a wealthy man who lived happily with his three sons in a mansion with a big garden. In the garden there was an apple tree, which provided not only big red and juicy apples but also one big golden apple per year. The big golden apple was sold to provide the family with income and more wealth—until one year when the owner made his way to pick his golden apple of the year and noticed that it was gone.
>
> Confused and angry, he called for a family meeting with his sons and shared his concern with them. The oldest son suggested that next year one of them should keep watch and guard the golden apple until it was ripe enough to be picked.

They all welcomed the idea, and the oldest son promised his family he would be the first to stand guard.

The following year, on the day and night chosen by the father, he made his way to the garden, sat under the tree, and watched the sky until it darkened. He ate some of his packed food, tried to keep his mind occupied, and tried to focus on the issue and whatever trick he could find in his books to stay awake and alert, but soon the boredom and sleep got hold of him and he fell asleep.

He woke up at dawn and found out that the apple had been stolen again. Embarrassed, he made his way to the house and explained it all to his father. His father, who was disappointed in his oldest son, relieved him of his duty and delegated the responsibility to his middle son for the following year.

The following year the middle son, burdened with the huge responsibility of finding the thief and pleasing his father, came up with new tricks to stay awake—singing, thinking of upsetting things, and walking around the tree rather than sitting under it. None of these tricks proved helpful as he too fell asleep and woke up before dawn to the realisation that this year's apple had also been stolen from right under his nose.

Disappointed in himself, he approached his father and told him of the news. His father, who knew that he could not afford to lose another golden apple the following year, realised immediately that he needed to think of a better and more effective solution.

Going in circles with his thoughts, his youngest son approached him: 'Father—please allow me the opportunity to catch the thief next year.'

'Your two older brothers have already tried without success. You are far too young, and I cannot risk our fortune another year.'

'I will not fail you! I promise that I will bring the golden apple back next year. The thief will not get away on my watch.' With that promise and a bag of hope, he was given the honour of catching the thief.

He was the youngest, wittiest, and wisest of all three. He was determined to catch the thief in order to prove himself to his family and gain his father's respect. When the time came, he made himself a pack containing a knife, salt, and clean cloths.

His mind wandered as he sat under the tree, watching the sky and the golden apple, but soon he focused again and started to walk around the tree. At sunset he felt tired and hungry, which kept him awake, but around midnight he could barely keep his eyes open—and that is when he turned to the resources he had assembled.

He opened his pack and cut his finger with the knife. Then he poured salt over the cut, which made him scream with pain. Finally he wrapped the finger with a clean cloth and sat in pain. He repeated this action every time he felt sleepy. At last he heard leaves rustling in the apple tree above him. He closed his eyes, snored, and pretended to be asleep.

'This is the third year that the silly owner sent his son to catch me, but he has no clue that I was carefully chosen by the Deeve himself because of my reputation for being the best thief in the land,' the voice said.

He opened an eye to catch a glimpse of the thief in action and saw that the best thief in the land was nothing but a big black bird. He waited silently until the bird was ready to fly again. The boy decided to follow the bird and rose to his feet when he saw it fly towards the east with the golden apple...

"Shirin Jaan! Time to wake up! The car is already here!" Maman bozorg gently whispered in my ear.

It took me a couple of minutes to figure out where I was, what I was asked to do, and for what reason. "The story?" were my first words.

"You fell asleep halfway through."

"You have to tell me the rest!"

"Shirin Jaan, the bags are already in the car. Everyone is waiting."

"I can't leave! I need to hear the rest of the story! I have to!"

"There is no time, Love. I give you my word—the next time we see each other; I will tell you the rest. Something to look forward to, hey?" Maman bozorg said with a smile.

I started to cry. I wanted to hear the rest of the story and I wasn't prepared to leave. I wanted to scream and shout and basically throw a tantrum. *But what good will it do?* I thought.

"Listen to me, Shirin—you need to be strong for your mother and your brother. They count on you. Your mother will rely on you for support. Be a big girl and remember to stay brave. My final advice to you would be to be strong and grateful, no matter what life throws at you." She gave me a kiss on my forehead and wiped my tears.

"Shirin Jaan!" I heard my mother knocking at the bedroom door.

"We are coming," I said quickly, while deep down yearning for some more privacy with Maman bozorg.

I don't remember ever having to be woken up that early in the morning. It was still dark, obviously before dawn. I dressed quickly, and when I opened my bedroom door, I realised that I only had a couple of minutes to say goodbye. To my surprise, I felt relieved about that. I quickly kissed the immediate family members, in denial of whom and what I was saying goodbye to. I sat in the car, and as we pulled away I said goodbye to our house, to our road, to our local bakery shop, local supermarket, to my school, and to Tehran.

I had never seen the streets of Tehran so empty of traffic and people. Perhaps it was my imagination, but I had never seen Tehran look so charming and delightful. As the sun rose, I looked out through the back window of the car and, with tears in my eyes, thought of Maman bozorg's words: "…be strong and grateful!"

And so I was! I was strong and grateful when our *Nowroz* was covered with snow that year, without any sign of spring in Sweden. I was strong and grateful when I was asked sarcastically at school how many camels my father owned, and asked when I was to go back to my own country. I even tried to be strong and grateful when we were told that my Maman bozorg had passed away, shortly after we had left Iran. I promised to stay strong and grateful when I realised that I might have to live with the unfinished story for the rest of my life.

Epilogue

An afternoon breeze gave me the excuse to escape reality and move to the window.

Looking out, I could see children playing in the playground, with their mummies in sight. Some were rushing to catch buses home, some had just started their evening with flowers in hand, waiting for a loved one. Shops were closing and restaurants were opening. It was a pleasant afternoon in the city of Uppsala, and everyone wanted to enjoy the day while it lasted.

"Can you see your dad coming?" my mother asked.

"No," I said, pretending as if I was looking for him amongst the crowd.

"He should have been back by now," she said with a sigh.

"You shouldn't have asked him to buy a guitar case," I argued.

"How else were you supposed to take the guitar with you to London?"

"I wouldn't! I have survived without it for so many years. I don't have to take it home."

"How sad that the original case disappeared in the move," she sighed again. "But your dad will buy you a better one." She paused, then said, "Come here, sit next to me." She moved her legs to offer me a seat.

Reluctantly, I turned around.

There she was, lying in bed with morphine dripping in her veins, bringing her pain relief from the cancer that had spread so fast and resided in most of her organs. It was painful to witness. I wanted to look away, close my eyes, and have a slide show of the past, hopes for the future, just to escape this scene.

"Is there anything I can do for you? Head massage, foot massage, some ice cream?" I asked desperately, wanting to give her some comfort.

"Actually, there is something you could do for me," she said, catching my attention immediately.

"Please tell me!" I said hurriedly.

"Tell me one of Maman bozorg's tales," she said pleadingly. "You remember them, don't you?"

In all the years after we had left Iran, we had never spoken about them or retold them, so I had to think for a moment.

"My only regret is that I have not written them down for my grandchildren," Mum said, interrupting my thoughts. "Promise me that you will."

"Let's not think about that now. Let's think about you surviving cancer, holding the children in your arms, and telling the tales like Maman bozorg used to for us. Now, which one do you want me to tell you?"

"Promise me that you will write them down, Shirin."

"I promise!" I said quickly, just to change the subject.

"Yeki bood, yeki nabood," I began.

Lightning Source UK Ltd.
Milton Keynes UK
08 December 2010

163978UK00002B/14/P